## A MESSAGE FROM CHICKEN HOUSE

A crew of street children, a pet bushbaby and a missing mum – there are plenty of things to discover in this heart-warming, uplifting, toe-tapping modern-day adventure set in Nigeria's largest city. Will TV's *Lagos Let's Dance* set them all on the path to discover their true destiny? Or will harsh city life rob them of their dreams? Efua Traoré is the best at real-life stories where hope always finds a way!

**BARRY CUNNINGHAM**
Publisher
Chicken House

# ONE CHANCE DANCE

## EFUA TRAORÉ

Chicken House

2 Palmer Street, Frome, Somerset BA11 1DS
www.chickenhousebooks.com

Text © Efua Traoré 2023

First published in Great Britain in 2023
Chicken House
2 Palmer Street
Frome, Somerset BA11 1DS
United Kingdom
www.chickenhousebooks.com

Chicken House/Scholastic Ireland, 89E Lagan Road, Dublin Industrial Estate,
Glasnevin, Dublin D11 HP5F, Republic of Ireland

Cover and interior design by Micaela Alcaino
Typeset by Dorchester Typesetting Group Ltd
Printed and bound in Great Britain by CPI Group (UK) Ltd, Croydon CR0 4YY

FSC
www.fsc.org
MIX
Paper | Supporting
responsible forestry
FSC® C171272

1 3 5 7 9 10 8 6 4 2

British Library Cataloguing in Publication data available.

PB ISBN 978-1-915026-50-7
eISBN 978-1-915026-73-6

Also by Efua Traoré

*Children of the Quicksands*
*The House of Shells*

# CHAPTER 1

# WHEN YOUR POT OF LUCK IS EMPTY

Jomi loved picking up abandoned things. Things people threw away, calling them useless.

*Nothing is ever truly useless* was his favourite thing to say, when he found something lying about.

Every single thing had a use somewhere inside of it, even if it might not be obvious at first sight. Anyone who was good at fixing things, like Jomi, knew that.

Jomi's favourite place in the world was the scrap hill outside the village. It was a hill of treasures. The first time the truck came to offload scrap at the back of the village, all the grown-ups turned into angry bees, buzzing about the mound of scrap until late into the night. The next day they went to complain at the town council. But no one listened to them. No one listens to poor people.

And so, the trucks kept coming. And Jomi didn't mind because he began discovering all sorts of gems between the scraps. People crinkled their noses when they saw the cracked phones, broken strollers, rattling keyboards, ruptured TV screens, scrunched-up cans and plastic bottles. They didn't see what Jomi saw. The copper wires, magnets, wheel bearings, switches, DC motors, batteries and thousands of other goodies. All ready to be fixed and shined up and used to build something new.

And the treasure hill was right outside their house. Jomi didn't even need to cross valleys or climb mountains or sail away on a ship like a pirate to find the treasures.

He'd sewn extra-large and extra-strong pockets that went all the way down to his knees so he could fill them up with lots of amazing stuff. Stuff people had abandoned.

Sometimes it was tough. Fixing things, or

making new things out of them. Like this tin car he'd built with a little sail in front and a fan motor behind to make it drive faster.

'Come on!' Tinuke cried, her long braids dancing. 'Show us what you can do.' His cousin was his biggest ally.

Jomi screwed the rubber wheel back on. This car was his best yet. Or would be, if it didn't keep crashing.

He joined back the wires to the rusty battery he'd found at the scrap hill. The car staggered forward but this time it settled into a slow, smooth drive.

'Ha!' Tinuke cried and quickly popped the little iron lady she'd built into the car. The lady fit in perfectly and rattled along with the car, until it hit the leg of the table on the veranda and both crashed upside down.

'Did you see how she drove the car?'

Jomi gave her a high five.

'I told you, you need little iron people for your cars and luckily for you, you have me to supply you with them!'

Jomi picked up the car and set it right. He

smiled at the mention of luck. He'd learnt a new word at school today that was even better than luck. And it had made him excited, his whole body gripped by a vibrating energy all afternoon. It was this really long, weird word that had curled off their tongues strangely and made them laugh as they repeated it in English class.

Serendipity.

Mr Bola had said it was a very special kind of luck. Ordinary luck was what happened while you were trying very hard to do or find something and you got lucky. Just like searching for scrap on a hill. But serendipity was the special luck that happened when you weren't expecting it. When you weren't doing anything to find it and just got lucky out of the blue.

Jomi had immediately thought of his mum when he heard this. He remembered her bright, dreamy eyes filled with excitement. *Don't look too hard, Jomi*, she would say. *Don't even let life know what you are after. Just go about your business and then suddenly life will surprise you.* How he would have loved to tell her this word, serendipity. It was made for her.

The car began moving again. He was so absorbed in watching it jerk and rattle across the dusty veranda that he didn't hear the steps approaching. Suddenly a shadow loomed over them.

Jomi froze.

'Welcome Mummy,' Tinuke said, quickly jumping up and helping her mother remove the large basin she was carrying on her head. Jomi gulped down his shock and scanned the front yard frantically for the broom he'd dropped somewhere.

His aunt stretched her back and shook out her arms to loosen her muscles after carrying the heavy basin all the way back from the market. And all the while, her eyes were on him, slowly eating him up.

He managed to find his voice. 'Welcome Aunty Patience,' he mumbled.

Her scowl eased and her twisted eyebrows straightened. He wondered if he might just get lucky this time. But unfortunately, his car chose that moment to bump into Aunty Patience's foot.

She looked at it, bent down slowly and picked

the car up along with his instruments, which lay scattered at her feet. Jomi's muscles went limp. She inspected the car briefly, shook her head and then she squeezed it. The thin metal broke with a mournful creak that cut through his tightly wound-up insides.

'But Mummy,' Tinuke cried as she watched the iron lady clatter to the ground and lose her head.

'Get inside,' Aunty Patience barked at her. Then she grabbed Jomi's ear and pulled him forward. He yelped.

'How many times have I told you to stop playing around with this rubbish, when there are things to be done in the house? Have you washed the clothes I put out?'

'Yes, yes Aunty,' Jomi cried, tears squeezing out of the corners of his eyes.

She let go of his ear. 'And why did you not sweep the yard like I said?'

'I was just about to,' he mumbled, rubbing his ear.

'Get along with it. I am tired of feeding you and not getting anything back for it. You will work for your keep in this house and make yourself useful! Have you heard?'

He stared at the dusty red ground beneath his bare feet and nodded.

'Now, fetch me a bucket of water from the well, for my shower, and then sweep the yard!'

Jomi stumbled towards the well at the back of the house, his heart feeling like it had swapped position with his stomach. But it wasn't because of the wicked throb in his earlobe. It was because of what Aunty Patience still held in her hand. He glanced back and watched her grip his pliers and scissors tightly as she walked into the house.

## CHAPTER 2

# WHEN YOUR HEAD DOESN'T QUITE FIT ON YOUR SHOULDERS

**W**hen Jomi's mother left, everyone said she would never return. Especially Aunty Patience, who was the wife of his mum's older brother. 'She is lazy!' Aunty Patience had said, hissing loudly, her lips twisting in disgust. 'Too proud to do honest farm work like the rest of us!'

Everyone agreed his mum's ori never fitted quite right on her shoulders. It was always looking this way and that or dreaming away high up in the clouds, too far away and too big to fit well on her slim shoulders.

But Jomi knew better. His mum had told him the story of Ayanmo, which means destiny. Ayanmo determines all human lives. Before their births, the lifeless bodies of humans are sent to the keeper of the ori, to choose their heads. Each person chooses their head, the most important part of their body. It is a heavy, life-defining choice after which they are sent to the stream of forgetfulness out of which they are born. If a person chooses a good ori, then they are one of the lucky ones who will have a good destiny. If a person chooses a bad ori, then they'd end up poor like Jomi and his mum.

But Jomi's mum had sworn to him that her ori was not a bad one. She said her destiny was just sleeping and she had to go in search of her, to poke her and wake her up.

Jomi knew she would never abandon him because she'd told him that on the night she'd left. He remembered the smells and sounds of that night clearly. The busy chatter of hawkers and passengers at the bus stop, the scent of his mum's cocoa-butter hair cream which had made her freshly braided hair shine, making her look even younger than she already was. The glow in her eyes and the sound of her warm, excited voice as she spoke.

'Jomi,' she had said. 'You know why I gave you your name, Oluwajomiloju?'

He had nodded eagerly.

'Because you are the first surprise that life had in store for me when I was only fifteen. You were my biggest and only surprise yet.' She had laid an arm around his shoulders and pulled him closer, not minding that his face creased and dirtied her Sunday dress which she'd put on for the journey.

He'd snuggled deeper into her embrace and listened to her heart beat fast along with her words.

'There has to be more to life than what we have here,' she had said, whispering. 'I know I have a bigger purpose. I'm like one of those scraps on your scrap hill.'

Jomi had looked at her in surprise and she'd grinned and nodded her head vigorously, her braids forming wavy shadows on her face in the dim light.

'Lying around there on a scrap hill, each part is useless. But when shined up and put together with the right piece, the scrap becomes useful and those wonderful toy cars that you build emerge. That is how it will be for me. Do you understand what I am trying to say?'

He had nodded and she'd squeezed his hand.

'I knew you would be the only one to believe me,' she had whispered, then kissed the top of his head. Her warm breath had smelt of lemon and ginger and he had inhaled all of it.

'As soon as I have put together enough money and found a place for us, I will come and get you from your uncle and aunty. I promise.'

And then swinging the small nylon bag of her few belongings on to her shoulder, she'd squeezed into the rickety bus that was brimming with travellers, bags, sacks, cartons and loud squawking chickens in big baskets. The bus that would take her to Lagos, the city of dreams. Dreams that floated around every corner. You just had to snatch one for yourself.

Ducking her head beneath sweaty armpits, tall headties and bulging bags, she had disappeared and was gone.

Jomi had remained behind, standing in the middle of the empty bus stop, until the sound of the coughing bus engine and the trail of black smoke had disappeared.

# CHAPTER 3

# WHEN AN ENTIRE FOREST DISAPPEARS IN ONE DAY

'**O**ur forest o! They are taking down the forest!'
The screams came from all ends of the village. Jomi and Tinuke dropped their forks of fried plantain and eggs at the very same time. Uncle Babatunde jumped up with a grunt and stormed past them. A second later, they were running out of the house and after him.

The bulldozers worked mechanically and relentlessly like a locust invasion on a cornfield. From a distance they almost looked like toy cars driving over little farms and hills, felling trees, crumbling cocoa pods and smashing green pineapples to pulp as if they were nothing.

Even the villagers, their eyes wide and bulging, mouths hanging open, fists pumping in vain, looked unreal – like little iron people.

It was on this day of the bulldozers that Jomi finally understood why his mum had left.

Even though his memories of her were now like crumbs on a plate – so few that it was difficult to say what meal had been eaten – Jomi still believed in her. Even though she'd never written, like she had promised, he trusted her and held on to his little crumbs of memories. But it was the day their world was turned upside down by the bulldozers and the villagers were scattered about like weevils out of a sack of old beans that he'd really understood.

The truth was that, here in this village, they were nothing. They were poor and unimportant, like wriggling worms in the hands of a playful child.

Jomi spent the day watching the bulldozers, fascinated in a bellyaching kind of way. The mighty machines climbed over bushes, mounds of earth and even hills as if they were just having an evening stroll. One tree after the other fell as easily as elephant grass sliced down by a sharp cutlass. From morning till late afternoon, he watched, hypnotized. He could not help himself. Wheels and motors were the most exciting things in the world. And anyway, it was better watching the destruction site than watching his aunt and the other women wailing and wiping tears off their faces with their headties, or watching his uncle and the other men in the village shouting at the stony-faced leader of the bulldozer men. To no avail. The villagers were dripping with sweat from yelling and exhaustion, but the leader of the bulldozers with his bright yellow helmet and huge earphones remained unbothered. He seemed totally oblivious to the angry and desperate villagers as he commanded the bulldozers to do their job.

More kids joined Jomi at the edge of the site of destruction.

'Wawu! Look at that huge one climbing over the hill there!' someone called.

'Gbosaaah!' one kid cried as a rosewood tree crumbled, looking majestic even while breaking.

'Scattah!' another kid yelled as a palm tree fell to its knees, spilling red palm kernels like drops of blood.

Some little ones even clapped in glee, not understanding.

A swarm of bats swooped out of the forest. They fluttered overhead, briefly darkening the sky and then dispersing into the greying distance – beginning the search for a new home. Shrill squeaks followed, ripping through the air and through Jomi's brain. Panicking bush pigs.

Suddenly he felt ill. Sick and tired of the noise of destruction and of standing in one spot all afternoon. It was gradually getting dark and the whole scene was beginning to feel ghostly.

The truth of what all this meant for the village and for the wild animals was beginning to hit him.

He kicked a stone so hard, his foot hurt. Then he limped away towards the scrap hill. He usually went there every single day but today the shocking events had upturned everybody's routine. It was almost too dark to search for scrap now but he would go anyway. It was the one place that always made him feel good.

A swift movement ahead caught his attention. A small dark shadow rushed out of the skeletal remains of the forest and crossed the dirt road. It disappeared into a round mound of earth.

Jomi hurried forward, wondering what animal it was that had been scared out of its habitat. The mound of earth was a calabash. The round, hollowed-out gourd had been half buried beneath the dirt by the bulldozers when they'd passed there that morning. He went down on his knees and peered into the slender neck of the gourd.

The brightest, largest eyes he'd ever seen were staring at him.

Jomi jumped backwards in fear. Scrambling noises came from within the calabash. He'd scared the animal.

Quietly and slowly he crept back to it.

'Don't be scared,' he said gently.

Just then, a loud crack went through the air as yet another tree went down. More panicked scrambling in the calabash and a tiny, frightened sniffle.

'So sorry about that,' he whispered. 'And sorry you lost your home. I know how you feel. I also don't have a home. Well, not one that is mine at least.'

He took down his rucksack from his back and groped through his collection of wires and batteries and other odd things he had gathered. He always carried his rucksack around with him for fear that anyone – mainly Aunty Patience – might steal or throw away his things.

'I am going to shine some light now,' he said as soon as he found his torchlight. 'Please don't be scared, I just want to have a quick look at you to see if you are OK.'

Carefully, he shone the light not directly into the calabash but just over the mouth of the gourd. Then he peered inside. It was difficult to recognize anything. All he saw was a fluffy, dark brown bundle of fur.

The furry bundle unfolded and again huge bright eyes stared at him. Large ears unfurled and rotated backwards.

Jomi gasped. 'Wow! I think you are a bush-baby! I have never ever seen one of you in real life. Your kind are always so shy, always hiding away in the forest and only coming out at night.'

Loud calls joined the rumble of the bulldozers. The leader of the bulldozers with the yellow helmet was shouting something to one of his men, and the man in turn ran towards the bulldozers waving and shouting.

The bulldozers all began to turn around, moving through the huge expanse of chaos and wasteland they had created and back towards the leader.

'Oh, I think they have finished,' Jomi said with a sigh of relief.

But then the first of the bulldozers crawled on to the dirt road and began heading towards him.

He tried to pull the calabash out of the ground but it was stuck.

'Oh no, quick,' he hissed at the bushbaby. 'You have to come out. The bulldozers will crush you in there!'

But the bushbaby, immediately sensing his panic, folded its ears down over its eyes and curled back up into a furry ball.

'No!' Jomi whispered, glancing back at the bulldozers. They had formed a long, curved line of destruction that looked like a boa constrictor slithering forward to attack.

# CHAPTER 4

# AN UNEXPECTED FIND

**M**others yanked babies out of the path of the heavy bulldozers. The children who had been standing with Jomi earlier squealed and scrambled off the dirt road.

Jomi began to dig around the calabash frantically. His fingers hurt as he clawed away at the earth. It was hard and dense.

The huge vehicles were already closing in on him and his heart was almost choking him with its loud drumming. He grabbed the slender neck of the calabash and tugged, but it was still too deep in the earth. It was now completely dark and he wasn't sure they could even see him kneeling on the road. He would be crushed by them and they wouldn't even notice!

Jomi waved his hands but the bulldozer didn't

slow. He dug into his deep pockets. Now he wished they weren't so full! It took him for ever to find his wooden pincers – and even longer to scratch and poke the earth with them. This time it worked better and some more earth gave way from around the belly of the gourd.

'Get away from there!' a voice boomed. 'Who is that? Do you want to get killed?'

'Someone stop the bulldozers!' another voice cried. 'There is a child in the way.'

But the bulldozers ploughed on. Jomi could now feel the heat of their engines at the back of his neck. The dust they raised blurred his eyes and clogged his throat. A layer of sweat sprouted out of his back from the sudden wave of heat and the fear. Just at the moment the first bulldozer reached him, the earth finally gave way. He fell backwards and out of the way, a shriek of terror escaping his lips. In his arms he clutched the calabash tightly.

'What a stupid child!' a voice said. Jomi ignored this and pushed the gourd into his ruck-sack. It just managed to fit in on top of his things, only its open mouth sticking out. He carefully strapped the rucksack on to his back and hurried back towards the village. It was definitely too dark for the scrapyard now.

Maybe he could coax the bushbaby out with some crumbs of food. What did bushbabies even eat? What would they find to eat in the forest? This one was probably about the size of a small cat. Did it feed on seeds or wild fruits or maybe insects? Bigger ones like moths or large spiders? Or maybe it ate mice or other little animals?

The sounds of the retreating bulldozers were only a low rumble in the distance now. The villagers remained in huddled groups, discussing the terrible events with tired voices. No one noticed him as he made his way back to the house.

It was dark and abandoned. Thank goodness. He needed to see what to do about the bushbaby before everyone came back.

He rushed through the front door which to his surprise stood wide open. They'd all run out when the bulldozers arrived and obviously no one had bothered to come back home since then. No one had worked or eaten or swept their houses today. No one had done anything other than watch the bulldozers break down the foundations of their lives.

Jomi closed the door behind him with a sigh and hurried to the kitchen. He lit a kerosene lamp and found the bucket that he and Tinuke had filled with cashews the previous day. They'd found a new tree in the forest that had been bursting with fruit. His belly lurched. The tree was now gone.

Very carefully, he took his bag down. The bushbaby must have already caught the scent of overripe cashews because scratchy, eager sounds came from within.

Jomi picked up a cashew and held it at the mouth of the gourd. A small, furry paw snatched the fruit from him. He grinned and popped the bushbaby another one. Then he slid his hand slowly inside the neck of the gourd and waited. Soon he felt a wet, sniffy snout tickle his fingers.

'We have to find a hiding place for you,' he said quietly. The others would soon return.

He grabbed the kerosene lamp and his bag and was about to hurry to the room he shared with Tinuke when he stopped in surprise. Aunty

Patience and Uncle Babatunde's bedroom door was wide open. Aunty Patience never, ever left the door unlocked in her absence.

His breath snagged. He could literally just walk in and get all the things that she'd seized from him over the years. If she had kept them, that is.

This was too good to be true. He peered out of the window and when he was sure that no one was coming up the road, he hurried into their bedroom.

'Sorry little bushbaby,' he mumbled quietly. 'I just need to do something before I take care of you. It won't take long.'

He left the lamp in the corridor and groped his way through the darkness. She would see the light from down the road, if she were on her way back. If she discovered him in here it would be the end of him. He searched her drawers, listening for clanky sounds when pulling them open. A clatter of his pliers or scissors, or of the star screwdriver she'd seized last Christmas when he hadn't been careful enough. And the roll of black tape that he had been so pleased to find. Frayed at the edges but still sticky enough to hold things together.

Nothing clanked. No metallic sounds.

Had she thrown his things away? Was that the reason she always ignored him when he asked for them? He slammed the door of her wardrobe shut. She had no right! They were his things!

A panicked, scratchy sound in his rucksack reminded him that he was not alone.

'Sorry, I didn't mean to scare you,' he whispered to the bushbaby. 'Just one last thing.'

He dropped the rucksack beside him, searched for his mini-torchlight in his pockets and then sprawled himself on the ground in front of the bed. He could make out a large squarish shape. He shone the torch on to it. It was a pretty grey wooden box with blue flowery prints on it.

He pulled it out carefully and clicked it open. And there, rolled into an old cloth, were his tools.

'Yes! Yes!' he whispered again and again as he discovered even things he'd forgotten about. Like his solar-powered torchlight, which someone had thrown away because they thought it was broken. Jomi had placed it under the sun for some hours and it had worked again. His compass! He'd thought he'd lost it. He stared at them longingly, but knew he couldn't just take them all. If she checked the box and saw the things were missing, then she would immediately know it was him. He sighed. He would just allow himself to take only one or two things. Hopefully she wouldn't notice.

While he tried to make up his mind between the compass, the tape and his pliers, he glanced at the other things in the box. A framed document caught his eye. A kind of certificate. He took it out and shone his torch.

### *Admission letter.*
We hereby congratulate Miss Patience Akande on her admission to St Andrews School of Nursing and Midwifery, Lagos.

Hmm. Jomi frowned as he stared at the framed admission letter. He hadn't known that his aunt had ever gone to nursing school. That she'd ever been to Lagos. But why had she framed an admission letter? Usually people framed their certificates of successfully finishing school and not of being admitted. At least that was what his head teacher had done. There was a framed picture of his teaching college certificate on the wall in his office.

He peered back into the box and that's when he saw it.

A slim pack of three folded papers that looked like letters, tied together by a rubber band. He held the pack up to the light and his breath snagged at the words written in bright blue ink – 'My dear Jomi . . .'

## CHAPTER 5

# WHAT IS MINE IS NOT YOURS

Jomi clenched the letters to his belly. 'Mine!' he hissed. A dark, fuzzy thing was filling up his chest. He could feel it taking up all the corners and spaces.

Slowly he loosened his fingers from the letter. He stared at the words that had been meant for him but had been hidden here in a flowery box instead, fading and gathering dust. He tried to read them, but the letter was trembling so much the words shuddered and floated out of sight. He should get out of here first and read it in peace somewhere else.

In one swift movement, he snatched up his pliers and then his scissors, the one-armed tweezer, the compass, the torch and the tape. 'Mine!' he repeated again and again, and stuffed all of them into his pockets.

He shut the box and pushed it back under the bed. Then he carefully picked up the rucksack and hurried to the room he shared with Tinuke.

'I knew you didn't forget me,' he said in a ragged whisper. He sat on his bed and scanned the letters for the one with the oldest date. It was almost three years old. She had written him just a few weeks after she arrived in Lagos.

My dear Jomi,

How have you been? I think of you every day and wish I could have taken you with me. But do not worry, the moment I have saved enough money to afford a place for us both, I will come for you. Promise!

Lagos is just like I imagined! It is loud and busy and bursting with colours and heavy with smells, each one trying to outweigh the other. Lagos never rests. You just need time to adapt to it. Trying to make a life here is like dipping your hand into an endless pool of muddy water in which treasures are hidden. It might take a while to find your treasure and some people may have to dive deep inside the mud while searching. They might get dirty and muddy or even stuck, but everyone has a fair chance of getting one of those hidden treasures. Is that not amazing?

There is a show here called *Lagos Let's Dance*. It is a dance competition on TV and it has me shaking my waist and twirling around every time I watch it. Remember that day we danced behind that tall bus parked on the roadside? The music from the radio called us and we just danced in the rain. We didn't care that the people in the bus were grinning at us, with their noses pressed into the back window. We felt the music in our bones, didn't we? We danced out all our worries that day. I think that is my destiny. To become a dancer.

Tomi, I have exciting news already. I think Ayanmo is already showing her face, our destiny is starting to take shape. After only a few months here, I already have a job. I clean one of these fine-fine houses with big bushes of white hibiscus in front. The house is huge and the work never finishes but the pay is good and I have a place to stay and food to eat. The madam has been so kind to me. I have calculated that in two years, I should have put enough money together. Then I will come for you, my lucky charm. I miss you.

Your Mummy (Ayanmo's true daughter)

Jomi drew a deep, shaky breath.

She was all right. She had found a job and had a wonderful madam. And she hadn't forgotten him.

Of course she hadn't forgotten him! He was a little ashamed of that thought. She'd promised him and yet recently the thought had begun to worry him, like a fly worrying an open sore. The thought had kept buzzing into his mind and each time he'd shushed it away, angrily.

But then why hadn't she come for him after two years, like she'd planned? Now three years had gone by and he was still here. With shaky fingers he moved on to the next letter. The light of his torch dwindled to a feeble glow and died. Argh! He hurried out to the kerosene lamp in the corridor and holding the second letter to its light, began to read.

My dear Jomi,

I hope you are being a brave boy. Never forget what I told you. Ayanmo is only sleeping. When our destiny wakes up, everything will be as it was meant to be. I promise. Until then, be strong like a pillar for me. I can only be strong here, if I know that you are strong back home.

Over here, things have been going all right. Some days good, some days ~~bad~~ not too good. But that is how life is you know. If all days were good you wouldn't appreciate them enough.

Madam has been keeping my money for me. She says if it's all at the bank, it will increase and become much more at the end of two years. I hope it is a good idea to trust her completely like this. At the end of the two years she will pay me everything and I will come for you, my Jomi.

From the window of my room I can see a tall tower. At night it annoys me a little. It blinks broken red lights that keep me from sleeping. They seem to blink many words, but only two are bright enough to read: 'Send' and 'pity'. Can you imagine? Remember how I always said, I do not need pity in this life? People who wallow around in pity are weak people. That's why I came to Lagos. I want to wallow around in things that I have done that make me proud. And now these bright lights shine through my thin curtains every night as if they want to vex me. So I always cover one eye and try to blend out the 'S'. 'End pity' is much better don't you think?

*I guess you are angry with me because it is taking longer than you hoped. But please write me, Jomi, so I know you are OK. The address is on the envelope.*

*I miss you.*

*Your Mummy (Ayanmo's daughter)*


She thought he was angry with her!

A desperate sob stuck in his throat. 'Mum, I will write you,' he whispered, nodding hard.

But . . . where were the envelopes? He would need her address. There hadn't been any in the box.

Low voices trailed in from the darkness outside. Jomi stiffened and folded the letters quickly.

They were back!

# CHAPTER 6

# A HUNTER WITHOUT A FOREST

'I am finished!' Uncle Babatunde cried. He sank into his chair in the little living room and his head fell into his hands. 'I have become useless. What is a farmer without a farm? What is a hunter without a forest?' His voice was hoarse after a whole day spent shouting at the bulldozer men and discussing with the villagers.

Aunty Patience seated herself very slowly at the dinner table opposite him. Her back was straight and rigid as if it were being held up by an invisible stick. Her eyes were small and her gaze distant. Tinuke glanced at Jomi who was still standing at the door of their bedroom. They exchanged worried looks before she sat beside her mother. She fiddled with a new iron lady that she had built the day before. The room was heavy with shadows that the kerosene lamp had crowded into the corners of the room. The air was tense like when his aunty and uncle were having a fight.

Suddenly Uncle Babatunde jumped up and walked to his and Aunty Patience's bedroom with long, bristling strides. There were rustling sounds and then he reappeared wielding his cutlass that he usually kept in its sheath, well oiled and away from dust and rain. He marched to the front door, tore it open and flung the cutlass outside. It fell to the ground with a painful clatter that made them all jump.

'Children! To your room,' Aunty Patience hissed.

Jomi hurried into their bedroom. Tinuke followed, closing the door behind her. The scratching sound of a match was the only sound and then the lamp beside her bed flamed up.

'Maybe finally you will wake up to reality.' Aunty's voice carried through the slit beneath the door like a treacherous harmattan wind. It was cold and surprising, sneaking under the door and curling icy fingers around Jomi. He shivered.

'Maybe now, you will listen to me and go to the

factories in town. Maybe you will finally look for a real job there instead of holding on to your farm as if you cannot live without it. Just because your father and forefathers were farmers and hunters does not mean you have to hold on to your cutlass like it is a part of your body.'

Uncle Babatunde grumbled something incomprehensible.

'All the sensible young people have long since gone to get jobs there,' she continued.

'What is wrong with holding up traditions?' Uncle Babatunde asked. 'What is wrong with being proud of what I am and what I have?'

'What you have is nothing! What is there to be proud of?' Aunty Patience snapped.

Tinuke cringed beside Jomi.

There was a stony silence from the other side of the door.

'You are heartless, wife.'

'I am only being practical. And make sure you take Jomi with you. There will be work for him there. Just tell them he is fourteen or fifteen, but small for his age.'

'What? But he is only twelve! Are you suggesting I should take the boy out of school?'

'Of course! Do you think we can still go on feeding and clothing him? We can barely feed and clothe our own daughter. We've sent him to primary school. That is enough education, especially considering the circumstances.'

'But Wande left him in my care!'

'She had no right to leave him with us when we were barely getting by ourselves! And besides, she promised to be back a year later. Have you seen her head inside this house in the past three years?'

Silence again.

Tinuke glanced at him. Jomi didn't meet her gaze; he could feel her eyes burning holes of pity into his skin and it stung. He immediately understood the words in his mum's letter. Pity was bitter and embarrassing. He hated it.

'She has forgotten her own child,' Aunty Patience continued.

Jomi crunched his fingers into fists. His mum hadn't forgotten him. She had written, like she'd promised. But a thought had been butting into the back of his mind since he'd read the letters. Why were there only three letters? And why had she still not come for him, three years later? She'd said she would need only two years.

'That is what Lagos does to people,' his aunty continued. 'It swallows people with its dangerous city charm.' Her voice had gone soft, almost wistful. 'Nobody who goes off to Lagos ever comes back. I should have gone when I had my chance. I should have gone for my training as a nurse.'

Her voice had hardened again and she thrashed out her words at Uncle Babatunde.

'Instead I stayed and married you. I let the opportunity slip away just like the earth of your farm has slipped out of your fingers today. Maybe now you can understand how I have felt all these years.'

Suddenly, a terrible piercing cry tore through the house. It was weird and sad and haunting. Jomi's skin tingled, his legs weakening. The sound was so close he could feel the cry vibrate in his chest. It came from the corner beside his bed where he had dropped his rucksack earlier.

The bushbaby!

He had completely forgotten it.

The bedroom door tore open. Aunty Patience and Uncle Babatunde rushed in and Jomi was startled out of his stupor. He darted to his rucksack and peeked into the open mouth of the calabash.

'Shhh,' he whispered.

Immediately the crying stopped.

'It's OK,' he said quietly. 'Everything is OK.'

Weird squeaky, snuffling noises came from within the gourd.

'What in heaven's name is that?' Aunty Patience cried. 'Do you have a baby in there?'

Jomi reached a hand into the gourd to let the bushbaby smell him and hopefully calm it. He felt something soft and wet around his fingers. He smiled and pulled his hand out slowly.

The creature immediately popped its head out.

'A bushbaby!' Tinuke whispered. She knelt down beside Jomi. 'Oooh, it's so cute.'

It really had the largest eyes Jomi had ever seen. They were like round buttons of honey-coloured liquid. They didn't seem to be able to move in their sockets, because it moved its head slowly from him to Tinuke and then back to him. The way he imagined a live teddy bear would.

Another loud scream ripped through the air.

This time it was Aunty Patience.

The bushbaby dived back into the calabash with a speed that surprised Jomi.

'Get. That. Thing. Out. Of. This. House.'

Her voice was a hoarse half-choke as she moved backwards towards the door, her eyes wide.

'Babatunde, get rid of it!'

Jomi jumped up and stood in front of his rucksack, shielding it from her view.

'I . . .' Jomi gulped. 'I found it. It lost its home now that the forest . . .'

'These things are devilish spirits! They bring bad luck,' Aunty Patience stuttered. 'They take away your riches, your wealth . . . how could you bring it into my house!'

'Calm down, Patience,' Uncle Babatunde said. 'Those are just myths.'

'They are not myths. I heard they drive you mad with their cries . . . oh my Lord, I should have covered my ears. We should have all covered our ears . . . we will run mad!'

Uncle Babatunde sighed and turned to Jomi. The wrinkles that crossed his forehead looked deeper and longer than usual. He jerked his head in a tired gesture towards the door.

'Please, just get rid of it quickly, OK?'

'But there is no forest left! Where should I take it? It doesn't have a home.'

'I don't care,' Aunty Patience boomed. 'Out with it!'

'Mummy—' Tinuke began. But she was cut short by her mother's stern look.

'Now!' she repeated.

Jomi picked up his rucksack. Scratchy sounds came from within the calabash. His heart hung heavy at its hinges as he slowly walked towards the front door.

# CHAPTER 7

# A DECISION THAT CHANGED EVERYTHING

'That useless boy will be the end of us,' Aunty Patience muttered, not even caring that he was still at the door and could hear her. Her words clogged his throat like the tangy fumes of burning wires and plastic on the rubbish piles he scoured.

He was choking on them. He wanted to escape from them. From her. He wanted his mum.

He gripped the door handle tightly and turned to face his aunt.

'Why did you hide her letters from me?' He pulled them out of his shorts pocket and held them up for his aunt to see.

'What . . . Do you mean you were sneaking through my things?'

'They are mine! She wrote them to me!'

'Wande wrote?' Uncle Babatunde had just started to sit down in his chair but stopped in mid-air like a broken robot.

Aunty Patience's eyes darted between her husband and Jomi at the door, back and forth as if she was thinking hard how to get out of the situation. But Jomi folded his hands across his chest, waiting, and Uncle Babatunde looked like he wanted an immediate answer as well.

'There was no need to keep the boy's hopes up for nothing,' she snapped. 'That's why I told the post office boy to stop bringing her letters here!' Her voice was still as sharp as ever, even though she sat down slowly, shrinking into herself.

Jomi gasped. There had been more letters!

'That was not your decision to make. You are not his mother.'

'In her absence, I *am* his mother and I took the decision in her place.'

'I could have written her,' Jomi cried. 'I could have told her to come back. Now she thinks I am angry with her because I never replied.' What if she thought he didn't need her any more? Cold shudders ran down his spine at the thought.

'How could you, Patience?! I would also have liked to hear how my sister is faring.'

'As soon as I read all that talk about big fancy dreams of becoming a dancer I knew she was just a dreamer. A spoilt, lazy person who would never own her responsibility. I did it for you, Jomi, and for you, Babatunde. You would only have been disappointed if you had kept your hopes up.'

'That was not for you to decide. You had no right to deprive the child of his hopes and of the little he had of his mother, even if it was just letters about dreams. How could you? I know you have always been jealous of her. You have always been bitter. Since the day we married. But even then, how could you do that, Patience?'

'How dare you?' Aunty Patience cried. 'After all I have done for your sister, taking in her child as if he were mine. This will all end today.'

'What are you trying to say?' Uncle Babatunde asked, his voice suddenly sharp.

Tinuke came up to Jomi at the door and slipped a shaky hand into his. Tears glistened on her cheeks.

'Be very careful what you say now,' Uncle Babatunde warned. 'We have had a terrible day.

Maybe we should continue this discussion tomorrow.'

'It is OK,' Jomi said, his voice trembling slightly. 'I know things will be tough around here now that the forests and farms are destroyed. I don't want to work in the factories. If I'm to leave school anyway, I'd rather go to Lagos and look for my mum.'

Jomi felt his bones stretch a little as the words left his mouth, making him feel taller. Yes, that was what he would do. He was going to find her.

'Oh, look at this one!' Aunty Patience waved her hand around at him, like he was a piece of scrap on a hill. 'How do you want to find her? You don't have an address. She made sure not to write an address on the envelope. She was afraid we would send you to her, if we knew it. She didn't want you to come!'

'Yes, she did. She wrote the address on the envelope,' Jomi cut in. 'She even asked why I didn't write to her. But you threw the envelopes away, so I couldn't, didn't you?'

Aunty Patience didn't reply. She just fidgeted uncomfortably in her seat.

Uncle Babatunde stared at her as if he were seeing someone he didn't recognize.

'It doesn't matter,' Jomi said quietly. 'Ayanmo will bring us back together.'

'Forget all that Ayanmo talk. Didn't you read the third letter? She has given up and finally accepted her fate. And besides, you would never find her in Lagos. Where would you even start looking for her?'

Jomi shook his head and stumbled out of the door.

Tinuke tried to hold him back but he prised his hand out of hers. 'I'm sorry,' he said, shaking his head sadly at her.

His uncle's and Tinuke's voices calling his name were like invisible ropes trying to pull him back. He struggled but pushed forward.

'He'll be back, don't you worry,' Aunty Patience cackled. 'That useless boy is not going anywhere.'

His aunt's voice ripped the last invisible rope holding him. And even though he felt like he was unravelling and disintegrating with each step, Jomi ran away as fast as he could.

## CHAPTER 8

# A HOMELESS BUSHBABY AND A HOMELESS BOY

The forest, which had stood and breathed at the break of dawn, was now a wide empty space, as still as death. It was an endless stretch of grey, a void with dark shadows of chaos and destruction at its feet.

The air was heavy with the tangy scent of spilt tree sap, broken bark and crushed leaves. It smelt of the last dying breaths of the fallen trees that lay in a messy criss-cross over each other.

Jomi sank down on to a ragged stump. His chest rattled like a broken radio as he opened his bag with trembling fingers. The bushbaby immediately popped its head out and twisted it almost all the way round. It knew where they were.

Looking like a furry ball in the dark, it leapt

out of the gourd and high into the air with no noticeable effort. Jomi gasped when he discovered it metres away on the branches of a fallen fruit tree. It was already snatching up little green fruit from the branches and stuffing them into its mouth.

Jomi sighed. The bushbaby already had a plan. Stuffing its belly full. What was his plan? What would he do now? How had he come up with this preposterous idea? He couldn't just go off to Lagos. First of all, he didn't have any money to his name. He'd just given away all his savings for that roll of copper wire he'd bought on market day last week.

But he had to find her. A surge of fear rushed through his veins at the memory of his aunt's words. *Didn't you read the third letter? She has given up and finally accepted her fate.*

What had she meant by that? He was already pulling out the letters from his pocket.

It was too dark to read. The sky was dense with clouds. His torch batteries were dead. Jomi thought quickly and began to dig in the sides of his rucksack. The solar torch he had gotten back would be of no use yet. He would need to charge it in the sun first. He felt around until he found what he was looking for. His bag of old batteries. He just needed them to work for a minute. He slid two into the torch and tested them. After the third set, it worked and the torch flickered a dim beam of light.

Quickly he began to read.

*Dear Jomi,*

*I hope all is well with you and that you are working hard in school. I know one day you will make me proud.*

*Unfortunately, I have bad news. Madam is not as kind as I thought she was. She keeps trying to delay giving me my money. Every day another excuse. Today she tells me this, tomorrow she tells me that. Now she wants me to work another year for her. I do not trust her. But I cannot leave because she owes me money for two years of work. If I leave now, then everything I did up till now would have been for nothing.*

*I am worried, my Jomi. And I wish you would write.*

*Sometimes I wonder if I should forget about Ayanmo. What if she has forgotten us? Or what if I chose a bad ori after all? Maybe I do not even have a* better destiny planned out for me. What if it is my destiny to remain poor? What if it is my destiny to remain separated from you?

But I don't want you to worry about yourself though, I am sure you have a better fate planned out, my Jomi. Sometimes I wonder if you might be better off without me.

I do not know it. It is hard to know things any more when my head is heavy with worries.

Your Mummy (~~Ayanmo's daughter~~)

The torch had gone out and still Jomi sat there staring at the outline of the letter.

The bushbaby was scrambling about, popping fruit into its mouth, cracking the seeds and munching loudly. Jomi finally looked up.

He glanced past the space where the forest had been and beyond. For the first time he could see the lights of Ijepa in the distance. Without the forest, the town was now in plain sight. His breath caught. That was where he needed to go first.

Jomi got up and glanced at the busy bushbaby, his jaws clenching. He searched the distance to the left. The bulldozers had parked on the other side of the village, where in the following days, they would erase the rest of the forest all the way up to the towns beyond. To the right the scrap hill stretched out, blocking the view of the highway that led to the towns in the other direction.

'I have to go,' he said. 'My mum is in trouble. She needs me. I need to find her and remind her of something. Will you be OK?'

The bushbaby glanced up, its large eyes reflecting the moon that peeked briefly through a gap in the curtain of clouds. It cocked its head and its eyes observed Jomi closely. Its gaze was intense, almost as if it understood him. Its eyes seemed to contract and they suddenly looked deeply sad. Jomi felt his cheeks burn with shame at his question.

Of course the bushbaby wasn't going to be all right. It didn't have a home.

Jomi snatched up his bag. He didn't have a home, either. But he just had to believe that he would be all right. He had to find his mum and together they would find a new home.

The bushbaby would have to do the same. He

swallowed.

'I'm sorry,' he mumbled. And without glancing back, he turned his back on the animal and made his way around the forest and towards Ijepa.

It was the last Friday of the month.

The lorry that came in from Lagos once a month would have arrived today in the afternoon. It was no coincidence that it was today. That had to be a sign. He was sure of it. Was it a sign from Ayanmo? That special luck his mum always spoke about, the luck you weren't expecting.

Serendipity.

Jomi began to walk faster.

The driver of the lorry always offloaded his goods and immediately reloaded his lorry with farming products from the villagers, which he would deliver to Lagos. He usually slept for a few hours and then headed back to Lagos in the middle of the night.

This was Jomi's one chance.

He arrived at Ijepa not long after, panting and a little worried. The town looked too quiet. Most lights were off already. Was he too late? His feet hurt and his rucksack was heavy with all the things he usually carried around with him. Every step he took shook the things in his pockets about, making a racket. He couldn't afford to call attention to himself. For his plan to work, he had to be quiet and stealthy like a leopard sneaking up on an antelope. He slowed down and swerved into the street that led to the bus stop. He kept to the shadows as he moved. The kiosk that was usually buzzing with crowds, cold drinks being passed in and out of it, was empty and crouched like a ghost guarding the car park. The hawkers who usually rushed around to sell snacks to passengers were gone and the entire space looked abandoned.

Just one lonely, bulky squarish shadow at the far end of the car park.

Jomi let out a sigh of relief. It was still there.

Goosebumps spread across his arms and up his back as he approached. He was actually going to do it. He would sneak into the lorry and go to Lagos. He would find his mum.

All of a sudden, a rumbling sound filled the quiet night air. The lorry shuddered to life and rear lights painted the road bright red.

Oh no! It was leaving.

Jomi began to run. His deep pockets, filled with all his gear, clattered against his legs. Would the lorry driver hear him above the engine rumble? Would he notice him in the rear mirror? Would he spot him in the dark? Jomi couldn't care; he had to catch up with the lorry, he had to risk everything.

The old lorry creaked into motion, tyres squelching over dirt.

Jomi ran harder – he was almost there. Just a few more steps.

With a last burst of energy, he caught up with it and lunged forward with one desperate leap.

One hand missed but the other caught hold of the latch at the rear. His body twisted and slammed painfully into the back of the lorry. He tightened his grip on the latch, caught hold of another and yanked himself up. His feet found a thin ledge. Slowly and with shaky legs like rubber, he straightened himself up.

He'd done it.

Suddenly something landed on Jomi's back. He stiffened in shock as it scrambled on to his shoulder. He yelped. The large round eyes of the bushbaby were staring at him.

'What are you doing here?' he whispered.

It chirped and Jomi knew the answer.

Just like him, the bushbaby didn't want to accept its fate. It wanted to find a better place, a new home.

He grinned and shrugged. 'But you have to be quiet, OK?'

The bushbaby made a weird clucking sound and he hoped it understood what it was getting into.

Jomi slipped in through the folds of the tarpaulin sheet covering the load area. The bushbaby slipped through after him and scrambled back into the calabash, which he still had in his rucksack. Jomi groped around in the darkness until he found a comfortable spot between what felt like sacks of flour. He lay back and stretched his limbs. It was going to be a long journey to Lagos.

# CHAPTER 9

# CITY OF NOISE AND SMELLS

Loud calls woke him. 'Agegeee . . . Ageegeee . . . Ojuelegba . . . Surulereeee . . . Pyiooo wootaaa . . .'

Jomi jumped up in a daze, his heart thrashing at the sudden rumble and racket.

He jerked around, rubbing his eyes to see better in the dim light. Big brown sacks of yam flour, cartons of yam tubers and round baskets of cocoyam huddled together looking like dejected stowaways. The night came rushing back. He'd run away. He was on his own, without a coin to his name. And he was the stowaway.

'Hey, bushbaby, are you awake?' His whisper was a brittle croak and his throat felt parched. He hadn't even thought to bring something to eat or some water. Goodness, what kind of a runaway was he? He'd started off without a single plan, not even a drop of water in case he got thirsty.

'Are you awake?' But there was no scrambling or movement from inside the gourd. He slid a hand inside. No nuzzling or wet snout? He looked around. He was completely alone. It seemed even the bushbaby had changed its mind and left.

The din from outside was getting louder. The tarpaulin sheets suddenly felt like a thin-walled prison, tightening around him, trapping him in the midst of a wild crowd. He covered his ears against the screaming hawkers, squawking chickens, bleating goats and bus conductors shouting their hoarse destinations over and over.

The lorry was slowing. Jomi jumped to his feet but immediately reeled over into a basket of cocoyam which crushed under his weight. The lorry swayed and the tarpaulin sheet creaked noisily as the lorry bumped through an uneven road. Jomi fell backwards and crashed back into the sack of yam flour he'd slept on. A ripping sound tore through the air, like old trousers when you overdid the splits. White yam flour fizzed up around him, blurring his sight. He'd burst the sack.

Jomi choked as the powder seeped into his nostrils and his throat. He breathed in short wheezy gasps, trying to throttle his impulse to cough and sneeze. But the more he gasped, the more of the powder seemed to fill his throat. He could already feel a huge sneeze gathering force. It prickled at the back of his nose, moved down to his protesting lungs, swelled up into a rush of tickles in his belly and then hurtled all the way back up. In one loud, explosive burst of a sneeze, he erupted.

Oh no! He sat rigid and still as a praying mantis, listening.

Could the driver have heard him through the engine buzz and the crowds around them?

The lorry jerked to an abrupt halt. A door slammed. Quick steps marched round the side of the lorry.

The tarpaulin sheet was ripped open and a smarting bright light like an electric spark blinded his eyes as sunlight crashed in. A waft of cool early morning air, heavy with smoke and fried akara, hit him.

'Wetin be dis? What the hell do you think you are doing in my truck!'

Jomi just stared at the man, wide-eyed and unable to move or speak.

The man's face was a twitching mass of narrowed eyes, a big pinched nose and tight-pressed lips.

'And what did you do . . . ?'

The man looked around the load area, inspecting the mess Jomi had made. Every single carton and basket was gleaming white; even the air sparkled white with the sunrays exposing the flour still floating in it.

'OK, you are in very big trouble young man,' the man said. He swung himself up over the ledge, lunging forward to grab Jomi.

'P-p-please . . .' Jomi stuttered. His knees had turned into two soft, mushy things.

Suddenly the man stopped, his hands stretched out in mid-air. His eyes widened and then he let out a weird shriek.

Jomi whirled around to see what he was staring at.

A white, hairy, goggle-eyed beast dangled off the roof of the truck. Its teeth were bared and its ears twirled backwards. The only thing about the beast that wasn't white were the huge reddish-brown eyes.

Jomi's heart lurched. His new friend hadn't abandoned him after all.

The bushbaby made a low but aggressive squeak and in one quick leap, sprang on to Jomi's shoulder.

The man howled and fell sideways on the sacks. More flour exploded into the air.

Jomi snatched his bag, lifted the tarpaulin sheet and scrambled out. He gasped at the sight. It was the largest bus-stop market he had ever seen, beyond anything he had imagined in his wildest dreams.

Crowds of people swarmed around big, bright umbrellas. Travellers laden with bags and boxes snaked alongside rickety orange buses in long, curvy queues. Bus conductors hurled the large bags into the buses, looking like giant ants carrying things double their size.

'Hold on tight,' Jomi whispered and hopped off the truck. The bushbaby gripped his shirt as if it understood. Its fur was still white and bristling and it looked around with eyes just as wide as his. Jomi landed with a wobbly thud and swung his rucksack on to his back. The bushbaby immediately dived inside.

Tyres screeched and Jomi looked up to see a yellow bus rumbling towards him. He leapt out of the way and began to run. Past rows and rows of trucks farting grey smoke into the air, and through bustling crowds of passengers. The ones wearing suits and fine-fine clothes were already looking hot and sweaty in the early morning sun. They were fanning themselves with newspapers or whatever they had. The ones in simple clothes like him didn't seem to mind the heat or care about sweating.

Water gathered in his mouth as he ran past an old woman roasting bole on a fuming stand. The brown plantains spiked into the air like dragon teeth, the grill pot the dragon's mouth spitting fire.

He darted past another woman stirring gleaming bobs of golden akara in a huge black pan of boiling oil. He eyed the hawkers carrying trays of refreshments on their heads and sighed. The trays were bulging with chunks of fresh pawpaw and pineapple wrapped in clingfilm, coconut slices dripping with cold water.

Jomi's neck was beginning to hurt with all the looking around. There was so much to see, so much happening at the same time. The smells alone were a whole new baffling world. How could so many smells mingle together all at once? They were as overwhelming as the sights. Tangy and sour and smoky and oily and fruity and peppery and sugary all at the same time. Like a ball of tangled-up wires which you would need an entire day to disentangle.

He stopped to catch his breath. The truck driver didn't seem to be chasing him – he could relax. He continued slowly now. His knotted insides loosened a little and the awe began to creep slowly into his body, filling his empty belly with hope.

Lagos was just like his mum had described. The sun had only just risen and the city was already alive and screaming and vibrating with energy. An excited heat throbbed in his bones. This was it. He only had to watch out for his dream floating around one of the next corners and then snatch it for himself. He was going to find his mum.

## CHAPTER 10

# TANKS (WITHOUT AN H)

'Commot for dia!' an angry voice shouted and something sharp shoved into his legs.

A wheelbarrow stacked with a swaying tower of plastic chairs prodded him out of the way. One angry eye glared at him through the chairs.

'Sorry,' Jomi mumbled, and jumped aside. He had to find a quieter spot to think and make plans. He looked around quickly.

Curious eyes were watching him. A kid with a slight sneer of a smile. Did they guess he was a runaway? Beyond the market, things looked quieter. He would go there.

Jomi squeezed through tightly packed rows of tables laden with vegetables, pyramids of rice, garri and other foods. He tucked his head into his shoulders and walked as fast as he could through the tunnel-like corridors. But nobody seemed to care here. Everyone was busy haggling prices or gossiping with stall neighbours. The rusty zinc roofs were so close to each other that they stopped any sunlight from coming in. The air was so thick and heavy and reluctant to move into his nostrils that Jomi had to swallow it down in big gulps through his mouth.

After rows of colourful cloth piles and some of jewellery, Jomi finally reached the end of the market and slowed down.

The stalls and tables here were shabbier. The roof sheets had holes, were broken or were missing and the sun crashed in. It was quieter in this empty part of the market. Oily plastic bags and crumpled shreds of newspaper littered the floor.

Not a person in sight.

Perfect. He would catch his breath here and then set up a plan.

Something he should have done earlier instead of just storming away and hopping on a truck to Lagos. How would he get food with no money? Where would he stay? Would he find a job? Were there scrap hills in Lagos? Maybe he could find something useful, repair it and sell it?

The thoughts stormed in, jumbling up his mind. His head began to feel heavy and his hollow belly tugged at him from the inside, making him feel all weird and dizzy. He kicked at an empty tin on the ground and immediately wished he was on his scrap hill, kicking up things to see what lay below. Searching for scrap always made him feel better. Finding broken things and making them useful again.

He scanned the corners of the empty stalls for anything he could pick up. An upturned basket caught his eye and he trudged towards it, flipping it with his foot to reveal its contents. Just empty plastic bags. He knelt down and poked around to be sure.

Nothing.

Approaching voices had him jerking up.

Some kids bounced their way into the market, giggling and arguing about something. The tallest one, with short dreads that sprouted off the top of his head like thorns, spotted him first. A smirk immediately formed on his lips.

'Omo, what the hell is that?' He pointed a

finger at Jomi. His voice was deep but a little squeaky at the edges, as if it had only just broken and still needed some oiling and practice. He looked maybe fourteen.

The other kids turned to stare at Jomi.

'This one na Egungun masquerade,' another kid said, slowing, but the others came closer.

Jomi tensed and backed into the moss-covered wall of the stall.

They gathered in front of him and began to laugh. The tall one with the dreads laughed so hard he had to hold his belly.

'You be ghost?'

Only then did Jomi understand why they were laughing. He hadn't dusted off the yam powder from his body. He began to rub and slap his arms roughly. His skin burnt from the slaps and from shame. How could he have been running around like this, all this while?

'Booo!' the tall boy suddenly hooted, shoving his face in Jomi's.

Jomi jumped and the kids laughed even more.

Jomi huddled into the wall, not caring how mushy it was.

'Leave him alone, Hassan!' a higher voice yelled. A smaller boy, wearing an oversized shirt with yellow suns and green palm trees over a pair of blue baggy shorts, pushed his way through. He adjusted his face cap which he was wearing the wrong way around.

'Or I'll tell Aunty Bisi,' he said, folding his arms across his chest and staring the big boy down. The others were all taller and older than him, but the boy didn't seem at all afraid.

'Chill,' the tall boy said. 'Just having a little fun with this loser.' He shoved his finger into Jomi's shoulder and Jomi fell back, his rucksack slamming into the wall with a hollow thud. The calabash!

A rush of scrambling came from within and the bushbaby popped out in a burst of white yam flour and chitter-chatter.

'Whoah!' The tall boy called Hassan fell on his bum and then began to scramble backwards. He looked like a crab with his thin legs and arms, scrambling all over the place.

The other kids ran away to a safe distance, half squealing, half laughing at the bushbaby and at the way Hassan had fallen.

'This is my ghost friend,' Jomi called. 'Bush-babies hate being woken from their sleep. Especially when they are hungry. You should never ever let them look into your eyes! If they know your face, they'll come find you at night and cry under your window.'

There was scrambling and a cloud of dust and then silence. The boy called Hassan and the others were gone, and only a trail of dust remained in the air.

Jomi let out a trembly sigh but went rigid when he noticed someone was still there in one of the other abandoned stalls, watching. The little boy with the palm tree shirt and baggy shorts was watching the bushbaby, his head tilted and wary. Suddenly, his face relaxed into a wide grin. Large, friendly eyes with long lashes crinkled at the edges. Something didn't quite fit.

Then Jomi noticed curled plaits pecking out from underneath the face cap at the back of her neck. She was a girl!

'So this is what a bushbaby looks like?' she asked.

Jomi nodded, his mouth also twitching into a

grin. The bushbaby didn't really look like one right now, with its white fur all bristly. It looked weirdly wrong, like a mixture of gremlin, teddy bear and monkey. He stroked its soft fur, twittering softly to calm it.

Its ears had swivelled backwards in alarm and its large button eyes scanned the stalls, its head twisting this way and that.

'That is the cutest pet I've ever seen.'

After a brief glance at the girl, the bushbaby snorted as if relieved everything was fine again. In one flash of a leap, it sprang into the air, twisted and disappeared into the folds of Jomi's rucksack.

Yam powder blurred Jomi's sight and he sneezed.

'What even happened to both of you? You really do look like scary Egungun masquerades.'

'We had a dramatic encounter with a sack of yam flour.'

She raised an eyebrow.

'I'm beginning to like her ghostly yam powder look though. It actually saved us twice now.'

'It's a she?'

'I think so,' Jomi said, realizing for the first

time that he'd just thought of the bushbaby as a 'she'. 'She just kind of feels like a friendly she.'

'What do you call her?'

Jomi shrugged. 'I haven't had her for long yet. We just met yesterday actually.' Had it really all just happened yesterday?

'But you have to give her a name! She can't just be nameless!' The girl looked horrified.

'Yeah, you're right. I've just not really had time to think of—' A thought flashed in his mind. 'Oh, I think I'll call her Ghost. Don't you think that fits her perfectly?'

Her teeth flashed and she gave him two thumbs up.

Jomi ceremoniously raised his arms and spread his fingers backwards towards the rucksack. 'I hereby officially name you, Ghost,' he called.

The girl pulled out a tattered notepad from her chest pocket. She twisted a tiny stub of pencil out of a rubber band tied to the notepad and began to scribble.

'What are you doing?'

'Writing.'

'I can see that. What are you writing?'

She looked up sharply.

Oh-oh, too nosy. Now Jomi wished he hadn't pressed her.

Her eyes narrowed but then her face softened.

'I'm making a list of special things that happen to me. But only really special things count. Things that don't happen to anybody on any random day. And when I reach a hundred, then . . .'

She bit her lip as if she'd said too much.

'So what special thing just happened?'

She opened her scruffy pad and turned it towards him. Jomi narrowed his eyes to decipher what she'd written. The last entry was number thirteen. She hadn't come very far yet.

'Oh, ehm sorry, can you read?' she asked.

He nodded and read out loud. 'Naming ceremony of a bushbaby.'

Jomi grinned and she did as well.

'OK, yes that's worth being on a list. Definitely doesn't happen every day.'

She glanced in the direction the boys had gone and began to walk away from him. Jomi felt a jolt in his belly. He badly wanted her to stay. To ask her what to do. To have a friend. And this little girl was so small and yet so brave. If only he could be like that too.

'That was brave of you, earlier,' Jomi said, trying to make her stay. 'And it was kind of you to help me.'

'No need for thanks, just call me by my name.' She pronounced 'thanks' like 'tanks' with a very sharp 't'.

'Ehm, OK . . . what's your name?'

'Tanks, of course.'

'Your name is Thanks?' he asked, raising his eyebrow. But when Jomi saw the look on her face, he wished he hadn't sounded so surprised. 'That's a ehm . . . nice name,' he added quickly.

Tanks bunched up her lips and scanned Jomi's face without replying, as if contemplating whether Jomi meant it or was teasing. But then she nodded.

'I know,' she said. 'But without h please. Tanks without h! I need to catch up with Hassan if I want any breakfast. He has our breakfast money.' She waved.

Jomi waved back.

'What's your name?'

'Jomi,' he called.

'OK Jomi, small piece of advice, you should wash your yam flour face and hair if you want anyone to take you seriously.'

And then she was gone.

## CHAPTER 11

# WHEN SIMPLE THINGS
# BECOME DIFFICULT

A shower and a meal.

Simple things that up till now he'd taken for granted were now the most difficult things to come by. If he had paper and a pencil – he did have them somewhere in his pockets, but he didn't feel like looking for them now – he'd make a list of all the things that he would love to have now. Things he didn't know if he would ever have again.

A shower and a meal would be number one and two. A drink number three.

Oh and feeling safe. That was number four.

A loud rumble echoed out of him. An angry monster had taken over his belly and was demanding to be fed. His last meal had been yesterday morning! He'd gulped down his fried plantain and eggs and run out to see the bulldozers. It felt like another life, another world, long ago.

He tried not to think of Tinuke. What she would be doing now. Was she thinking of him while she built little iron people?

The air in Lagos had to be thicker. He constantly had a burning sensation in his eyes, making the corners of them leak. Maybe it was the air pollution. All the cars everywhere.

He'd been trudging around for hours, dragging his feet over grey tarmac roads and red dusty ones. And everywhere Jomi went, there were people. After only a few hours in Lagos he was feeling dizzy from people and noise.

Finally, long past midday when he could hardly walk any more, he reached another somewhat smaller market. The scents of food were intoxicating and mind-fogging. But the best sight was a tap right in front of the market. A long queue of people balancing buckets and bowls of all kinds and shapes on their heads stood in line. But Jomi joined them, not minding the wait.

When it was finally his turn, he gulped down the water like a camel that had just crossed the Sahara. In between gulps he splashed his face and arms and washed off the yam powder.

'Oya-oya, you wan baff for here?' the woman behind him grumbled.

Before letting go of the tap, Jomi drank enough to drown the monster in his belly and finally it went quiet.

With new energy Jomi walked through to the back of the market towards a very familiar-looking hill of different-coloured, jutting-out shapes and objects. His steps quickened with growing excitement. But as soon as he reached it his shoulders drooped with disappointment. It wasn't a scrap hill. This was a real rubbish hill, stinking and fuming in the fire of the midday sun. He stomped up halfway, just to be sure there weren't any hidden treasures somewhere. But he began sinking deeper and deeper, his shoes making squishy noises as they smashed banana peels and squashed rotten tomatoes stuck in black, mossy plastic bags. Suddenly a dark spot in the heap shuddered. Then it jerked and growled. Slimy red eyes glared at him out of a scrawny pile of fur with more bald patches than hair.

Jomi darted down the hill and away from the mangy dog like a hundred-metre champion about to make a new world record.

The entire day turned out to be one big rubbish hill. As afternoon melted into evening, Jomi sunk deeper and deeper into despair. At the main road kids begged passers-by for money. They were small and thin and they darted around the tired-looking people in work clothes like busy flies, looking for something to eat. Jomi rushed to join them. He ran to a woman with a lovely hat and pearls around her neck and held out his hand, making a dejected face like the begging kids were doing.

'Get away from me you stinking brat!' the woman shrieked. She looked so disgusted that Jomi looked down at himself. His legs were nasty-looking, all the way up to his knees from where he'd sunk into the rubbish hill. He was even scruffier than the begging children. One of them glanced at him. He tried to smile at her, but she scrunched up her face and turned away.

A small woman with a round face and a heavy shopping bag on her shoulder passed by. She was munching and her fingers clutched a bag of chin-chin. She caught his eye. Jomi noticed how she slowed and his heart beat a little faster. She smiled at him and then dropped the chin-chin into his hand with a sorry kind of nod.

Jomi wasn't sorry at all. He munched up the whole bag in a few seconds. Never had chin-chin been so good.

It was only when he'd finished that he noticed how dirty his nails were.

He immediately felt queasy. Maybe he'd eaten too fast after not having anything for such a long time.

What should he do now? Why did everything seem so difficult? It was getting dark and he was tired of begging. This wasn't why he'd come to Lagos. He wanted to find his mum, not spend the day searching for food.

His eyes began to burn even more than ever. Was it the pungent air, the rows and rows of cars fighting their way through endless snakes of traffic? Or the different smells of the foods the hawkers were selling at the junctions?

Jomi rubbed his eyes and knew it wasn't the smells or the air. His eyes couldn't take it any more. He couldn't take it any more. His eyes broke loose and just cried and cried.

Could he give up? Could he just go back to Aunty Patience and Uncle Babatunde and Tinuke after coming this far? The truck driver had looked ready to give him a thorough whipping this morning. He was probably going to be checking his truck from top to bottom now to make sure there were no stowaways. Stowaways who broke his sacks.

Jomi wiped his face and tried to look for a corner where he could hide. But there was none. There were people everywhere, popping round corners, coming off buses and taxis, streaming out of every single direction he turned.

He ran down a narrow alley. He just wanted to get away from the noise and the crowds. The tall, thin houses were so close to a bridge for cars that arched in front of them, it looked like they were leaning into the bridge. The people living in them could shake hands with the drivers to cheer them up while they waited in the traffic jams.

The alley led underneath the bridge and became abruptly pitch dark. It smelt of pee and beer and old cigarettes. Little orange spots of cigarette lights dotted the dark. Shadows holding beer bottles huddled into each other, laughing with hoarse voices.

'Come here boy,' a voice croaked. A hand waved him over and suddenly all Jomi wanted to do was run all the way back to his uncle and aunty and Tinuke.

He turned around and ran and ran. His heart hit his lungs so hard it knocked the breath completely out of them. And still he ran. All the way back to the market he'd arrived at that morning.

The abandoned stalls where he'd met the girl called Tanks were quiet and empty and he drew a deep, ragged breath.

He'd hide here for the night.

And then tomorrow . . .

More tears fizzed out of his eyes.

He didn't want to think about what he'd do tomorrow.

# CHAPTER 12

# MIDNIGHT VISITORS

Scrambling noises startled Jomi. He sat up and rubbed his eyes. He'd dozed off the minute his head hit the green wall of the old stall.

The noises had come from his rucksack. Jomi relaxed and stretched his limbs. His body was a tired, aching, hungry mess. Like during yam season when they'd spent days on end helping Uncle Babatunde dig into mound after mound of earth to pull up heavy yams out of the ground. Only that then, after a long day of hard work, they'd been rewarded with thick slices of soft, fresh boiled yam dipped in palm oil and salt.

His belly monster was back and it was growling again. Ghost hopped out and on to his shoulder. He leant into her.

'I'm so glad you're here,' he whispered.

She began to lick herself clean, removing the last traces of the white flour on her brown fur. Jomi stroked her long bushy tail. It was as long and almost as wide as her entire body.

'Do you believe in things like destiny?'

Ghost carried on licking the powder, slurping it over her little pink tongue again and again. She seemed to be enjoying it.

'I really want to believe in Ayanmo. My mum does, you know. Or, well, she used to. I'm not sure if she still does any more.' Jomi sighed, his belly cramping.

'She used to believe that everything happens for a reason. Do you think we met for a reason?'

Ghost hopped off his shoulder and leapt across the stall on to the broken wall of the next abandoned stall. Then she leapt on to the roof and into a tree that glistened in the moonlit darkness.

'Yeah, you must be hungry too. Sorry I'm not the best caretaker. But I guess you're probably better at caring for yourself than I am.'

He made himself as comfortable as it was possible when lying on hard dirt and leaning into a slimy green wall.

*Don't get lost*, he thought but didn't call out the words. She'd followed him all the way from her ruined forest to the bus stop at Ijepa where he'd hopped on the lorry. He was probably more likely to get lost in Lagos than she was.

He watched her hop from one branch to the other. Sometimes she was Ghost, his bushbaby friend, bending the branches of a tree in the moonlight, and sometimes she was just a dark shadow flitting through leaves and he wondered if he was dreaming.

It had to be way past midnight now and he was so glad he'd come back here. All the action seemed to be taking place at the bus stop in front of the market. He could still hear music and voices and car horns in the distance. No one had come to this abandoned part since he'd set himself up for the night. Hopefully he'd be able to sleep here safely. He'd huddled close to the wall, hiding in its shadow, so even if someone passed by they wouldn't see him.

The distant sounds slowly lulled him back to sleep, but halfway between real life and dreamland he suddenly heard voices.

The voices came closer. He sat upright, his heart racing.

'I swear if you made us come out to this scary place in the middle of the night for nothing, then you owe us five puff-puff each,' a voice hissed.

'Stop being such an ajebutter.'

'I'm not being an ajebutter,' the voice hissed again in a sharp whisper. 'I heard gbomo-gbomo is on the loose again. This abandoned place would be the best place for them to hide.'

A snort.

Jomi pulled his legs to his chest and huddled deeper into his corner. His shoe made a loud swishing sound. Oh no! He must have dragged a piece of rubbish along with his foot.

Silence.

'What was that?' came a whisper.

'I don't know.'

The voices were directly in front of his stall now.

There was a clicking sound and a ray of light shone into his stall right in front of his feet.

Jomi's heart was pounding so loud, he could hardly hear their whispers.

'Probably just a rat.'

'Yeah, looks like the only thing we'll find here are rats.'

A sigh. 'OK, I guess I owe you both five puff-puff each.'

Why did the voice sound so familiar?

'Let's go.' Shuffling feet. The voices and steps retreated.

'Sorry guys. I really did have a very strong belly-feel this time, I swear.'

'You and your weird belly-feels.'

'I don't mind,' a third voice said. 'As long as I get paid puff-puff, you can wake me up any time of night to take me out for a stroll.'

'He was the cutest thing I ever saw though,' the familiar voice said.

Tanks! Jomi gulped and scrambled to his feet.

Three shadows were melting into the darkness outside the market. It had to be her.

'Tanks,' he called. 'Tanks without an h!'

The shadows whirled around.

'It's Jomi,' he called.

'Ha, you see! Told you guys,' Tanks said.

Jomi caught up with them.

'Hello,' he said.

Two boys stepped out of the shadows with Tanks.

'This is Jomi,' Tanks said.

'This is Prosper,' she went on, pointing to a small one, who leant heavily to one side.

'And this is Chuks.' The other boy was a little taller than her and very thin.

Jomi nodded, feeling too awkward to say anything.

The boys seemed just as shy because they just stared. Obviously, Tanks was the talker in their trio.

'Where's Ghost?' she asked, glancing at his rucksack.

Jomi pointed up at the tree, which had stopped bobbing. They were standing right under it now. Two bright eyes shone down at them. Ghost was watching.

'Hey Ghost, good girl,' Tanks called in a quiet whisper.

Ghost made some chirping noises in reply.

'We came to ask if you need a place to stay,' Tanks said, turning back to Jomi. 'You can stay with us.'

Prosper and Chuks both shot glances at her, their eyes widening.

'Really?' Jomi gulped. 'Yes, please,' he mumbled. And suddenly a rush of heat made his sore eyes tear up again.

Oh goodness! Not now, while they were all staring at him.

'We'll take you,' Tanks said. 'Will Ghost come too?' Her eyes scanned the tree eagerly.

Jomi nodded, not trusting his voice.

'Is . . . is she really a bushbaby?' Chuks asked, only snatching a quick glance at Jomi when he'd finished talking.

'Yes,' Jomi said.

'But how do we know she's not one of those monster ones that lure people into the forest at night with their terrible cries and take away all their riches?'

Jomi shook his head quickly. Not that he knew for sure; he'd heard enough weird stories about bushbabies. But since he'd met Ghost he'd not felt afraid of her a single time. She was his friend. He glanced up at her. She was grooming herself, pawing through her tail but eyeing them as she did so, as if she knew they were talking about her.

'Do we have any riches I need to know about, that should have us worried?' Tanks asked.

Prosper's and Chuks's teeth flashed white grins into the darkness.

'She does have a very weird baby cry though. Kind of a sad one,' Jomi said.

'Can you make her come down? Does she listen to you?' Prosper asked.

'I think so.' Jomi made a quiet, half-whistling, chittering sound. He'd learnt to copy animals from his uncle who had taken him into the forest a couple of times to hunt. He'd hated the hunting part but loved communicating with animals. Luring them by copying their sounds and then watching them.

Ghost immediately responded with a series of twitters.

He called again and she came, hopping down on to the roof and then on to his arm.

'Oh wow, that is so cool,' Prosper whispered and came closer with a slight limp. Ghost sniffed his hand.

'Bulldozers came and cleared away her forest.

Now she's homeless and I'm hoping I'll find her a nice new forest.'

Tanks looked up sharply. 'Bulldozers also took away my home,' she said quietly. 'They are mean devils.'

'I've never seen a forest in Lagos though,' Chuks said, venturing closer to carefully stroke Ghost.

'Oh,' Jomi said, 'that's . . . not good.'

'Yes, but you've not been everywhere in Lagos yet, have you?' Tanks said.

Ghost seemed to have had enough. She clutched Jomi's arm and jumped back into his rucksack.

'I think she still needs to get used to people. She lost her home just . . . yesterday.'

'OK, and we should really hurry back now, before someone finds out we broke the night curfew . . .' Tanks said.

Loud laughter and footsteps from behind them silenced her.

She glanced at the others. 'Now,' she whispered. And they began to run.

## CHAPTER 13

# A NEST TO SLEEP IN

'What is this person doing here!'

Jomi looked around in confusion. Bright sunlight glared relentlessly into the tiny room through a small window with cracked glass. His eyes burnt with the spray of light but his back hurt even more. He'd slept on a lumpy olive-green sofa that had a deep valley in the middle.

They'd sneaked in, in the dark, so he'd had no idea what the room he had slept in looked like. Some photos of earnest-looking kids watched him from photos on the wall. Just kids. Kids alone or together. No parents, no grown-ups and not much smiling in the photos. They looked so serious.

One of the faces suddenly leant out of the photos and into Jomi's face. Spiky dreads.

It was the boy from the day before. The mean

one called Hassan. He was as real as ever and was definitely also not smiling.

'I invited him here.' Tanks appeared in the doorway.

'Who allowed you to invite any new kid? You suppose ask Aunty Bisi first.'

'I will, this evening.'

'We no fit take in any new person at the moment,' Hassan said through teeth clenched as tightly as brand-new pliers.

'Says who?'

'Says Aunty Bisi. She no fit afford this place, or even food for us.'

'Well, we'll see about that.'

Tanks and Hassan were standing on either side of the sofa, their mouths pointed like the sharp beaks of cocks fighting over who would get the worm.

'I'm sorry, I don't want to cause a quarrel,' Jomi mumbled, but they didn't even look at him.

Tired-looking kids in skimpy singlets and old shorts trudged in. Tanks and the others had slept in the other room, which had to be the bedroom.

Prosper and Chuks came closer, their eyes

pinned warily on Hassan.

Jomi slipped out of his awkward position and stood up.

Hassan's eyes widened and he took a step back. 'This is na boy from the market yesterday!' he cried. 'You had that white little beast with you.' His eyes scanned the room, jerking from one corner to the next. 'Where is it?'

'Oh, you mean Ghost, his cute little pet that you and the others ran away from like squealing ajebutters?' Tanks said.

Hassan glanced at the other kids, and his face darkened.

'I . . . we did not . . .' he stuttered. 'Wild animals are not allowed for here. Aunty Bisi no go allow am.' Hassan stormed into the other room and slammed the door.

Tanks turned to face the others. 'Never mind all the beef and noise this morning,' she said with a forced smile. 'Everyone, this is Jomi. He is new to Lagos.' She glanced at him. Jomi nodded.

'I invited him here because he had nowhere to stay.'

Jomi stared at her. She was hardly as tall as he

was, was probably just twelve like him, but she was like a little grown-up.

'And Jomi has the cutest pet ever!' she squealed with a little jump.

OK, now she looked more like a toddler! He grinned.

As if on cue, there were scratching sounds at the window and a small brown furry figure tried to squeeze in through the metal window protectors.

The kids giggled and ran to the window.

Ghost's big saucer eyes had managed to squeeze through but the rest of her head and ears weren't cooperating.

Prosper and Chuks opened the front door and Ghost leapt in.

'Hey, how was your night in the mango tree?' Tanks asked gently, snatching her up. But then all the kids surrounded her and Ghost began to make nervous little chittering noises.

Jomi picked up his rucksack and walked over. Ghost dived in.

'She is nocturnal,' he said. 'She needs to sleep now.'

'What does nocturnal mean?' a little girl asked. She looked like the youngest of the bunch, probably about seven or eight.

'It means bushbabies are awake at night and sleep during the day. The opposite of us.'

'Oh,' the girl said, looking disappointed.

Tanks placed an arm on the girl's shoulders. 'Don't worry, Anna. Ghost will wake up as soon as it gets dark. So you can see her before your bedtime.'

'Why is her name Ghost?' Anna asked.

Jomi shrugged. 'It fits her, don't you think? She is a night animal, she can jump so far and so quickly that she looks like a spirit shadow jumping from tree to tree at night.'

'She is so cute,' another girl said. She stood beside a girl with exactly the same face. 'I am Taiwo and this is Keni, my twin,' she said. 'Welcome to our place, Jomi.'

'Thanks.' Jomi smiled as he carefully carried his rucksack outside. He would have to find a quiet, shady spot for Ghost during the day. Inside the house was too rowdy.

The entire bunch of kids followed him outside

into a tiny yard. The air was still cool and moist with morning dew and it was heavy with the scent of mango. The yard was walled all the way round with only a little gate that seemed to lead to the front of the house. One half of the small yard was stacked with cartons and sacks on some pallets and covered with tarpaulin sheets. The other side of the yard looked like the play spot. A tattered ball lay abandoned in a corner, old but still usable. And someone had drawn six circles into the sand to play Siwe. But the rest of the yard was taken up by a huge mango tree, one of the largest he'd ever seen. It stood right in the middle and just beneath it was a comfy-looking spot with two long benches, shady and cool, and completely sheltered by the tree.

There wasn't much of a hiding space anywhere in the courtyard. Apart from the stack of boxes and sacks and a large plastic drum to collect rain-water, every space was accessible and open.

'What are you looking for?' Prosper asked.

'I don't know where to put Ghost. She seems to like this calabash and I was looking for a quiet, safe spot for it.'

'We're not allowed to touch these things, anyway,' Tanks said, pointing to the boxes. 'They belong to Landlord. They're his things for his shop.'

'How do bushbabies usually sleep in the forest?' Prosper asked.

Jomi glanced up at the tree, remembering the night Uncle Babatunde had showed him a dark hollow, up in a tree trunk. A strange feeling ran through his belly at the thought of his uncle. He'd never really spoken much but he'd always been kind to him.

'Bushbabies and owls sleep in hollows like that one there,' his uncle had whispered, pointing to the hole in the tree. They'd been out hunting at night and while they waited for an antelope or bush pig, his uncle had told him things about nature.

'Every space and hollow in nature is there for a reason,' he'd said. 'In nature nothing is ever wasted.

'Birds and animals that can climb, eat the fruit up in the trees. And the fruit that fall to the ground are eaten by the ground animals. The spaces between big trees are filled by small plants. Even the barks of trees are useful. Some plants grow on the barks of trees; animals and insects live in trees. Nature is always balanced and each living thing lives in harmony with its surroundings.

'It is the humans who create an imbalance in nature. We take more than we need and we do not replace. We have forgotten that we are part of nature and born out of it. Look at this beautiful rosewood tree here,' he'd said, patting the trunk of the tall tree. 'In my grandfather's days, they were everywhere. But now we have to plant rubber trees everywhere because humans need rubber in industries. So now there is no more space for rosewood or anything else.'

His uncle had often reminded him of his mum. Thoughtful but hopeful, sure that life would work out if one believed in it. The same way that his mum had trusted in her destiny, so his uncle had trusted in nature. He had believed in the earth, the forest, in his farm and in his plants. But he had been right not to trust the humans. Now his forest was gone.

'Jomi? Where do bushbabies sleep in the

forest?' Prosper repeated.

He jumped out of his thoughts. 'Ehm, they make nests in hollow spaces in tree trunks.'

Everyone now looked up at the mango tree.

'There's no hollow up there. I know because we climb up to pluck the mangoes,' Tanks said.

'Yes, I guess Ghost would have also found it if there had been one. She'd probably have made herself a comfy spot to sleep already. But I have an idea. Does anyone have a rope or old clothes or shreds of cloth they don't need any more?'

'Ivie!' everyone called at once.

'Ivie works at a tailor, so she's always gathering and snipping old clothes and materials to practise on,' one of the twins said.

'I'll go ask her,' Anna said, running back into the house.

'I have a roll of tape somewhere.' Jomi carefully took out the gourd from his bag and placed it against the wall of the compound. Then he began searching through the bag, pulling out this and that.

'Wow, your rucksack is full of treasures!' Chuks gasped. 'It's like Ali Baba's cave.'

Jomi grinned. 'I guess Ali Baba's cave was a little more organized than my rucksack, though. I can never find anything in here.'

He dipped his hands into his pockets, groping around till his entire arms were deep inside them.

'Ahn-ahn, how deep are your pockets?' Prosper said.

Jomi grinned. 'I extended them by sewing on longer ones. Why should pockets always be so small? Who made that rule? They are so much more useful when they are deeper.'

'Haha, you are funny. Man, I like that,' Chuks said and offered his fist for a fist bump.

'Last night, I was wondering why you made such a racket with every step,' Tanks said. 'No wonder.'

'Ha, there it is.' He'd finally found his tape and even some elastic bands.

'OK, so this is the plan,' he said and began to explain how he wanted to build a nest.

## CHAPTER 14

# FOR NOW

The nest didn't really look like one, but it was perfect anyway. Anna had come back with a bag of cloth pieces from Ivie's collection. They'd weaved and knotted the ends of the old shreds of cloth to form a cord while chatting. Then with the help of the benches and an old rope which hung down from the tree, Jomi and Tanks had climbed up and found the perfect spot in the palm formed by four branches. They'd built a solid net of the knotted cloth strips between the four branches and then fitted and secured the gourd. Ghost had not popped out her head even once. She was fast asleep.

The others had gone back in when Jomi and Tanks came down. Only Prosper and Chuks were still sitting on the bench, waiting for them. They had gathered into a pile all the ripe mangoes that Jomi and Tanks had plucked and thrown down.

Now that Ghost was safe and taken care of, Jomi's mind filled back up with worries.

'Do you think Aunty Bisi will allow me to stay?' he asked.

Prosper and Chuks glanced at each other and Tanks scratched the back of her leg with her toe, not looking up.

'She is very kind though,' Tanks said.

'But what Hassan said is true,' Prosper said quietly. 'Aunty Bisi doesn't know how to feed us any more.'

At the mention of food, Jomi's belly suddenly groaned loud and long. His hand shot to his belly and he felt his face heat up. But no one laughed or made fun.

'Let's have breakfast,' Tanks said, marching off into the house. 'We have the remainder ogi from yesterday and look we have some early mangoes, hurray!'

The sweet-sour scent of ogi wafted through the living room. Water gathered in the corners of

Jomi's mouth even though he didn't really like ogi. After yesterday he would eat anything they gave him.

Tanks and Chuks heaved up a table that stood in the corner of the room and moved it away from the wall. Then they pulled out a stack of little plastic stools from beside it and lined them around the table.

One of the twins, maybe the one called Taiwo, came in from the little kitchen and placed a plate with thick slices of fresh mango on the table. Then she set cracked plastic bowls on each space.

Jomi looked around. Three of the walls of the room were a dull, yellowish colour. The photos of the kids and some posters and cards had been hung up in odd spots as if to hide stains and cracks. Only one wall, the one behind the table, was empty and painted completely black. Weird.

As if sensing the food was ready, the other kids all came in from the other room at the same time.

'Ivie made me a doll!' Anna rushed in, her eyes almost popping out of her face.

Everyone giggled.

'Why are you all laughing at me?' she said, her

lips puckering. She looked like she would cry any minute.

'You just looked like a doll yourself with your big eyes,' Chuks said, widening his own eyes.

'More like a bushbaby,' Prosper said.

'I'm not a bushbaby,' Anna said, folding her arms across her chest.

'Don't mind them, suga mi,' Tanks said, throwing an arm around her. 'Show me your doll.'

A tall girl appeared in the doorway, holding a tiny, colourful fluffy thing.

Anna plucked the doll out of her hands and pressed it to her chest.

The doll was a patchwork of dark brown cloth for its face and arms, sticking out sharply from beneath brightly coloured clothes. It was a little out of shape, as if the stuffing was too much in the belly and too little in the limbs, but that made it look even cuter and chubbier.

'Wow, Ivie, the doll is fine o,' one of the twins said.

The girl called Ivie smiled and twirled her hand around in a series of weird gestures.

'Yes,' Tanks said. 'The big belleh makes her

look cute and funny.'

'A doll to make me smile,' Anna said with a giggle.

Ivie began to gesticulate again. She made signs to the others that Jomi had never seen before. She was speaking in sign language! Her long fingers seemed soft and elastic like rubber as she swished them around. She also made some sounds Jomi didn't understand. Jomi watched her in awe. The others all seemed to understand her. It felt like they were all part of a secret, cool gang and he was the only one who wasn't a member.

Jomi felt a twist in his chest. How badly he wanted to belong here. He wanted to understand this language of the hands. He wanted to be able to stay here and have Ghost live in their tree until he found his mum. He crossed his fingers tightly behind his back. *Please let Aunty Bisi agree.*

'This is Jomi here,' Tanks said to Ivie.

Ivie smiled and nodded at him. Then she made some signs.

'Ivie says welcome,' Tanks said. 'And she can't wait to see Ghost.'

'Thanks. Yes, I'll introduce Ghost properly to

everyone tonight. Sorry she's a sleepy head in the daytime. Your doll is pretty,' he added.

She grinned.

'I helped her stuff the doll with grains of corn,' Anna added, looking like she would soon float away with pride.

'You chumped away most of the corn, that's why there wasn't any left for the arms and legs,' the twin said.

The other twin, Keni, came in from the kitchen and set a large pot of thick white pudding on the table.

Their chattering stopped and everyone sat around the table. Like Jomi, their eyes were hypnotized by the soft, thick blobs of ogi that Keni began to spoon into their bowls. She was careful, making sure the ladle was equally full each time she filled a bowl.

Jomi sat on the last empty chair, desperately hoping it was OK for him to just join their meal.

All eyes turned to him. 'That's Hassan's chair,' Chuks whispered. Jomi jumped back up.

'Hassan's gone. He's vexing and said he's not having any breakfast with us.' Taiwo shared a nervous glance with her twin. 'You can sit there, for now.'

The words *for now* echoed through the room. Jomi gulped.

'I won't need to stay long anyway,' he said. 'I came to Lagos to look for my mum. She works here and she is saving money for our very own place.' Jomi's heart swelled at the thought. He could hardly wait.

No one replied. Tanks was the only one who looked at him. Her eyes were strangely sad.

Jomi stroked the place in his shorts pocket where his mum's letters were hidden. The letters immediately made him feel better.

'As soon as I have found her, we will move together into our own place,' he said, forcing his voice to come out bolder. He needed to sound more convincing.

Tanks nodded. But her head bobbed stiffly and slowly as if she had to force it.

'Do you want to help us sell mangoes today, Jomi? We will need all the help we can get,' Chuks said.

'I want to help,' Anna cried.

'Shut up, Anna,' Prosper said. 'You'll go to the market with Taiwo and Keni and be a good pikin.'

Anna scowled.

'I'd love to help,' Jomi said, happy to change the topic.

Tanks clapped her hands and suddenly had a sly grin on her face.

'Are you a fast runner?'

# CHAPTER 15

# THE RUNNING GAME

'Selling is a game with simple rules,' Tanks said. She had to raise her voice to be heard above the uproar behind them.

'This,' she said, pointing to the wild traffic, 'is our field.'

Jomi's eyes widened. What did she mean? Cars swerved in and out of crooked traffic lanes, blowing angry horns, screeching tyres and blasting grey smoke into the air.

'Each run begins with eye contact,' Tanks continued. 'You wave your wares at a potential buyer and you watch closely to see if their eyes linger. The moment their eyes catch, you should already be running hard and calling your price. Don't ever let your buyer lose eye contact because you are too slow. The moment your buyer loses eye contact, the game is over. They have lost interest and you have missed your chance. Are you listening?'

Jomi nodded fiercely but he was watching a shirtless, wide-chested boy across the road. He dashed into the traffic and darted through the rows of cars, holding two bottles of Coke above his head, his upper body shiny with sweat. He moved like one of the players Jomi had once seen on TV in a game of American football. Holding up the ball, just before all the other players cornered him and crashed in on him. The cars closed in on the boy and suddenly Jomi couldn't see him. His breath caught and he craned his neck, his heart thumping. Where was he?

The boy's head popped out of the open car window into which he had stuck it. He no longer held the bottles and was racing back out of the traffic, dodging left and right like a grasshopper. In his hand he clutched scrunched-up money like a trophy.

Jomi's breathing eased but his belly was still a tight ball.

'Jomi, hellooo?' Tanks called into his face.

'Yes, yes.'

'As soon as you have eye contact, you should be running as fast as your interested buyer's car to hold their gaze. If you are lucky and the traffic is slow at that moment, then you will only need to walk fast or jog. If you are unlucky, and the traffic speeds up exactly at this moment, then you may have to run as if gbomo-gbomo is chasing you, or worse, you may have to give up.

'The most important rule of the game: never give your wares into the car or let go, if you are not sure you can run the race to the end to get your money. Always watch the flow of traffic so you know if it's fast or slow.

'The motto of Lagos traffic is *"no one brakes for no one"*.'

A big yellow bus roared past and Jomi squinted against the gust of hot exhaust that slammed his face. Colourful slogans criss-crossed the back of it and he read '*Every Man for Himself*' and '*Only God Knows*' before it rumbled out of sight.

'You don't want your buyer speeding off without paying, do you?'

Jomi shook his head.

'OK, then let the games begin,' Tanks said in a voice that reminded Jomi of his maths teacher trying to pretend that fractions and decimals were just as exciting as Sunday rice and chicken. Prosper and Chuks and Tanks formed a circle and all put one hand into its centre.

Jomi joined in even though he felt anything but excited, more like terrified. The others yelled, 'Ha!' and threw their hands in the air.

Prosper moved back to the side of the road where they'd already set up a rickety folding table and chair they'd brought along. 'I'm the home base,' he said, building a pyramid of mangoes on the little table.

Tanks and Chuks snatched up two mangoes each and ran to the edge of the traffic jam. Their eyes were sharp as torchlights with new batteries as they stared down cars and waved the juicy yellow mangoes.

'Finally, we have something to sell,' Prosper said, rubbing his hands together. 'We've been waiting for mango season since for ever. Now that Ivie works at the tailor and the twins weave hair at the market, we also wanted to do something to earn money.' Prosper looked really proud.

'Some weeks ago,' he continued, 'Chuks found money on the ground, so we bought four cold drinks from a road shop and tried to sell them in traffic. But before we managed to sell even one single bottle, the drinks were hot like steamy puff-puff because we don't have a cooler. And then we got into trouble with those ones.' He jerked his head towards the muscular boy. Jomi now noticed there were three of them. They were all darting in and out of the cars selling drinks. It looked like it was working for them.

'They stole our drinks from us and kicked us away. They said they are the drinks sellers. We should go find ourselves something else to sell.'

Jomi gulped.

'Then we tried offering to wash windscreens. But that didn't work either. We just kept on doing a lot of running for nothing.'

'Is there no other way to earn money?'

'It's the only way, unless you get lucky like Ivie and the twins and find a real job, or unless you want to join the area boys. That's what Hassan and his friends want to get into now. They're always hanging out with troublemakers. Aunty Bisi even got him a real job at a mechanic but he was back with his area-boy friends a few weeks later. If I should ever get a real job like that I would make sure to keep it,' Prosper said.

'Why don't we just take the mangoes to the market then and try to sell them there? Wouldn't that be easier?'

Prosper shook his head. 'We don't have a stall there. You can get into serious wahala for selling illegally. The agberos are always parading the place in gangs, kicking people out who can't pay them.'

Jomi sighed.

'You should watch Tanks,' Prosper said. 'She's the best because she's never afraid of anything.'

'It looks so dangerous.'

'It only looks dangerous the first time. Once you get used to it, it's easy.'

'Yeah sure,' Jomi said.

Prosper looked up sharply. 'Don't think I haven't done it before. I tried to run with the others. But I had to stop because I couldn't keep up with the cars. But don't think I can't run or that I'm too afraid or anything.'

'Oh, I didn't mean that you can't . . . I just . . . I can't imagine this getting easy for me. You lot are all so . . .' He swallowed. 'So brave.'

Prosper still looked wary. 'And just so you know, it's not that one of my legs is too short, it's cos my other leg is too long, that's why I limp. It's extra-long and strong.' Prosper glanced sharply at Jomi.

Jomi nodded.

'Look,' Prosper suddenly called, pointing.

Tanks was racing beside a shiny white car and holding the mangoes into the car window. But the window of the car suddenly rolled up and she yanked out her hand at the very last minute before the car jerked forward to keep up with the traffic. The car that was next in line blasted its horn at her and she jumped back out and on to the side-walk. Her face was glistening with sweat already and her small chest was heaving. She got back in line with Chuks at the side of the road.

'Sweet ripe mangoes!' she called along with Chuks. 'Juicy, ripe mangoes!'

Her eyes were on fire as she scanned the cars, watching for eye contact. She was already getting ready for her next run.

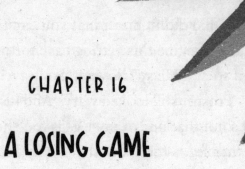

## CHAPTER 16

# A LOSING GAME

Jomi sighed. This game was madness!

But he owed it to them. They'd been so nice to him. The least he could do was help them sell some mangoes. He edged carefully to the side of the road. A loud blast of a horn had him scrambling back immediately.

If only he didn't feel like he was risking his life for this stupid game.

He took a deep breath and then began to scan the traffic. He held up his mangoes and waved them around. 'Mangoes! Sweet, juicy mangooooes,' he called again and again, like Tanks and Chuks were doing.

But no one was looking at him. This was frustrating.

He yelled louder but his voice came out hoarse

and he ended up coughing and clearing his throat for at least five minutes after almost choking. The air was too dirty and hot for all this shouting.

Chuks dashed in and chased a car for a few seconds but came back, sweating and out of breath. And still holding his two mangoes. This was never going to work.

No one was interested. They were all too busy driving.

*That's it!* he thought. He shouldn't be staring down the drivers. The passengers had more time to look around. He would see if he could catch their eye.

But there weren't as many passengers as drivers. Not all cars were brimming with people. And even the passengers were not always staring out at exactly the moment he was looking at them.

Suddenly another yellow bus passed. It was one of the big, rickety ones with lots of passengers, all looking very bored. It didn't have a door and through the entryway Jomi could clearly see a woman with an open book in her hands staring at his mangoes.

'Juicy mangoes!' he screamed. He wanted to

run in but the traffic was moving, so he ran on the sidewalk, parallel to the bus, until it slowed and there was a space in the road. He dashed in, swerved out of the way of a huge truck and crossed the lane. Now he was running beside the bus.

'How much?' the woman called, dropping her book into her lap.

'Fifty . . . fifty naira,' he gasped as he tried to keep up. His T-shirt was turning mushy under his armpits and sweat was skidding down the middle of his back as if it were a fun slide.

The bus slowed almost to a halt and Jomi saw his chance. He stuck one mango under his chin and with the free hand grabbed the long metal handle beside the missing door. With an action move that would have impressed even Spider-Man, he swung himself into the bus. The rusty ledge creaked and he toppled in head first.

His two mangoes hit the rusty floor of the bus and rolled away beneath the seats, all the way to the front. He watched them disappear and then looked up at the woman. She rolled her eyes and then went back to reading her book.

Just at that moment, a tall man at the front of

the bus got up.

'Hey, what is going on there?'

He stuffed the bunch of money he'd been counting into his big waist pouch. The bus conductor! He didn't look very pleased.

'I'm j-j-just selling mangoes,' Jomi stammered.

'In my bus? You dey find trouble, today?' the man growled. He began to squeeze through the bus, barrelling through the passengers and towards Jomi.

Jomi scrambled up and jumped out on the ledge, clawing the handle. But the bus was too fast. He couldn't just jump out now. He glanced up the road. It looked like they were reaching another tight spot, the bus would soon slow again.

But it was taking too long – the bus conductor had already reached him before the bus was slow enough. He reached out to grab Jomi.

Jomi ducked his head and the man's hand hit the door frame with a loud thud.

Now was his moment. Jomi leapt out, managed not to fall in front of a car and scrambled off the road just in time to avoid being crushed by a lorry that screeched to an angry halt.

He fell into a trembling heap at the roadside, right in front of the three muscled cold-drinks sellers. They sniggered.

'Oh, boy, you wan kill yaself because of mango?'

'Take am easy o!'

Tanks came running over, her face squashed into a big frown.

'Jomi! Are you OK?'

'I'm fine,' he mumbled, getting up quickly.

Chuks joined her and they glanced at each other. They didn't look happy.

'I'm sorry,' Jomi said. 'I lost the mangoes.'

'Jomi, the mangoes don't matter,' Tanks cried. 'They're not that important.'

'I wanted to help,' he said.

'Yes, but not by risking your life!' She looked really angry now. 'This was meant to be a fun game. Not a do-or-die game! We were just playing.'

Jomi felt foolish.

'Let's get Prosper, I think we should go home,' she said. 'And no telling Aunty Bisi about this. You know she doesn't like us near traffic.'

# CHAPTER 17

# AUNTY BISI

She was a tiny person, wearing large, black-rimmed glasses and a flowery dress with a small belt that hugged her slender waist. Why had he imagined Aunty Bisi as a tall, big woman wearing a buba and wrapper?

'Aunty Bisi! Aunty Bisi!' everyone chanted as soon as they heard the knock on the front door and the turn of the key. She was surrounded in an instant.

'Good evening children,' she said in a soft but firm voice. 'Is everyone all right?' She glanced at each of them, taking in the face and clothes of each and every single one of them and nodding while she did so.

She looked so young. Jomi felt a little disappointed. Could this tiny person possibly take care of all of them?

But there had to be something special about her. He had felt it all afternoon. In the way the kids had tidied the little house with a zeal that had surprised him. He'd sensed it in their excited high-pitched chatter, their eager fingers gripping broom, mop and sponge. Their twitching arms shaking out their cloths and pillows and folding them neatly on the mattresses they'd stacked in a heap to create space during the day.

'Where is Hassan?' she asked, immediately noticing that one of them was missing.

'He was here a minute ago,' Anna said.

'Hassan!' Keni called.

Aunty Bisi turned and caught sight of Jomi standing in the corner.

'Hello there,' she said, a small frown formed between her brows. 'We have a visitor?'

The chattering ceased and the room went quiet.

'Children, you know the rules. We have to keep safe. No visitors allowed inside. You can have friends and play with them, but not in the house.'

Prosper and Chuks exchanged worried glances and the others stared at the floor.

'I'm sorry to be adamant about this,' she said, turning back to Jomi, 'but these are our house rules. You may stay for dinner if you want but after that . . .'

Tanks stepped forward, looking awkward and fidgety in her large palm tree shirt and baggy shorts.

'Aunty Bisi, this is Jomi. I invited him in, I'm sorry, but it was the middle of the night and he had no place to stay.'

Tanks glanced at Jomi before continuing quietly. 'He just came to Lagos and doesn't know a single person. I couldn't just leave him out there, could I?'

Aunty Bisi sighed and rubbed her forehead but the frown remained and even deepened. She glanced at Jomi with eyes that suddenly looked small and tired behind the large frames of her glasses.

'OK.' She nodded. 'I'm not promising anything, but we'll see if we can find a way to get you sorted.'

'We don't have any space here for him!' Hassan popped his head into the living room. He was glaring at Aunty Bisi, his fists like tight rope knots. 'We are already too many and the food you bring is never enough!'

Gasps from around the room.

'Shut up, Hassan,' Tanks hissed.

Aunty Bisi just stared at him, her mouth open but no words coming.

Then she walked to the lumpy sofa and sank into it.

Hassan marched out the front door with large, angry steps. The door slammed behind him.

Aunty Bisi held out a bunch of keys. 'Can some of you get the food out of the car. Please lock the car afterwards.'

Her voice and her face were cleared of all emotions. No frown, no tight lips, no lines beside her mouth. Only a slight twitch at the corner of her eye. Jomi watched her closely, his heart thumping. *Please don't throw me out.*

The mood went back to happy and excited at dinner but Jomi couldn't get his throat to swallow. He shoved the rice around his plate even though his belly was empty and groaning.

They were all seated at the dining table. Aunty

had gotten an oil tin from the kitchen to sit on. She'd placed a newspaper over it to protect her pretty flowery dress.

As soon as she sat down, hands shot up in the air.

'Yes, Taiwo?' Aunty Bisi asked.

'Keni and I helped Madam do tiny million braids today. She said we did well and she bought us rice and moin-moin.'

'Wonderful,' Aunty said. 'Make sure you are always very polite, always greet well and speak good English to your customers like I told you. If they have a good impression of you, they will come back to you again and again.'

Chuks raised his hand.

'Yes, Chuks?' Aunty Bisi asked.

'I finished reading *Chike and the River*.'

'Wonderful, didn't I tell you you could do it? Well done. And did you enjoy it?'

Chuks grinned. 'Yes, Chike was cool.'

'Told you so!' Aunty Bisi smiled. 'Now Prosper can have his turn. If you have any problems Prosper, just ask Chuks and he can help you.'

Aunty Bisi glanced around the table. Almost all hands shot up again.

Jomi grinned in spite of his worries. It was like in school. Only that in school usually only two or three kids raised their hands while here everyone was dying to be called out. These kids here were eager and excited and wanted to impress Aunty Bisi or make her smile.

Anna's hand had been jerking this way and that, and was now going wild like the rotating blades of a helicopter.

Aunty Bisi smiled and nodded at her.

'I have the best news of all,' Anna cried. 'We now have our very own pet!'

'Oh, really?' Aunty Bisi raised an eyebrow. She didn't look like she believed it.

'Yes! We have a real pet, a bushbaby. Jomi brought it from his forest all the way to Lagos.'

Jomi's last bit of appetite disappeared as Aunty Bisi stared at him with a new frown.

Tanks rolled her eyes.

'Ouch,' Anna cried, peering under the table. 'Who kicked me?'

'It can sleep outside,' Jomi managed to say. 'We built a nest up in the mango tree. Bushbabies are nocturnal.'

'Hmmm,' Aunty Bisi said.

When dinner was over Aunty got up from the oil tin.

'Children, please clear the table and do the dishes and when I come back in we'll do our lessons.'

'Jomi,' she peered at him over her glasses before pushing them up her nose, 'why don't you and I go out into the courtyard for a little chat.'

## CHAPTER 18

# A TALK

The acrid smells of Lagos smoke and traffic had climbed over the high walls and penetrated the courtyard like invisible serpents. The smells and the loud city noises, so different from his village, were a sharp reminder of what was out there beyond the walls. Jomi's breath quickened. He didn't want to be back out there, alone and frightened. He wanted to stay here with the others.

Aunty Bisi was sitting on the bench and staring almost fearfully up into the tree. But her tight face loosened when she saw him approach and she smiled. A fresher scent of mango leaves and ripe mangoes pricked his nostrils as he walked over. He sat down on the bench opposite her and drew a long breath. The familiar smell wrapped itself around him like his old cuddly wrapper back home. The one that had belonged to his mum. Why hadn't he thought to bring it along?

'Your pet isn't dangerous, is it? Does it bite?'

'No.'

'What does it eat? We can't afford to feed it as well.'

'She feeds herself. I've seen her eat things like insects and worms and wild fruit.'

'No pets allowed inside the house.' She raised a finger. 'Understood?'

'Yes.'

'Now tell me about yourself, Jomi.'

Oh. Where should he start? What should he say? He stared at her feet. Her sandals were simple with brown straps and her feet were small and pretty and clean, not like his dirty ones.

'OK, no problem, I can start if you're not too sure yet. I'm Bisi, or Aunty Bisi as you already know. I'm twenty-eight years old and I work as a nurse as my main job. But I also do other side jobs like most people in Lagos.

'Lagos is a tough city, as you will probably soon find out if you haven't already.' The sides of her mouth turned down as she said this.

'I used to live here in this house with the kids, but a year ago I married and moved in with my husband. My plan was to have a caretaker to live here but unfortunately, that hasn't worked out yet.'

She looked away while she said this. She looked almost . . . ashamed.

Jomi wanted to make her feel better, but he didn't know how. How could she feel bad when she was being so kind to the kids?

'Why?' he asked.

'At the moment I can't pay someone to stay.' She still didn't meet his eyes.

'Oh no, ehm . . . I meant why do you help kids?'

'Oh,' she said. 'No one's asked me that before.'

She shrugged and then seemed lost in thought for a moment.

'Did you run away from your home?' she asked instead of replying to his question.

He swallowed. 'Yes. It wasn't really my home though. I was staying with my uncle and aunt and my cousin. But my aunt wasn't very nice to me and they couldn't take care of me any more. So, I ran away.'

'You shouldn't have,' she said quietly, staring into the darkness around them.

'I need to find my mum.' The words came out so sharply that she jerked up, her gaze back on him.

'Do you know where she is staying?'

He shook his head.

'I mean, do you have an address?'

'No,' he whispered. A tear escaped the corner of his eye. He wiped it away quickly but another one rolled down his cheek and into the neckline of his T-shirt before he could stop it.

Aunty Bisi moved over to his bench. There was only a little space between them and they just sat like that for a while.

'Don't worry, maybe we can find out where she is. Do you know what she's doing here? Is she working? Maybe the name of her employer? What part of Lagos maybe?'

'She works as a house help in someone's house . . . that's all I know.' His voice came out broken. Broken by the hopelessness of what he was saying. She probably thought he was stupid to come here based on only this information. He glanced sideways.

She didn't look disappointed or disgusted. Just sad.

'I won't lie to you, Jomi. It will be almost impossible to find her here. Probably twenty million people live in Lagos. And maids usually don't get registered into the system here. Unless your mum is one of the few maids employed by a placement agency. But I guess you wouldn't know how she is getting paid.'

'Oh yes, she mentioned she was being paid by her madam, the one she's staying with.' Jomi was relieved that he knew that. He looked up hopefully.

Aunty Bisi sighed.

'Oh, does that mean she won't be registered anywhere then?'

'Unfortunately, yes, that's what it means.'

Jomi felt his insides crumble. Had it all been for nothing?

'You would have been better off with your aunt and uncle. It's the worst thing to be out in the streets of Lagos as a kid. You are lucky Tanks found you.'

Aunty Bisi stood up.

'I guess I'll be taking care of you now,' she said. 'Don't worry, Jomi, we'll manage somehow.'

'Thank you,' he mumbled. Even though that was what he'd been hoping to hear, the heaviness in his chest didn't lift completely.

For now, he was happy to stay here. What he really wanted was to find his mum. But that suddenly seemed like a dream that had drifted further away and out of his reach.

As if Aunty Bisi had read his mind, she patted his shoulder. 'You know what, Jomi, hold on to your plan of finding her. I shouldn't have made it sound so hopeless just now. I . . . I just wanted to spare you . . .' She stopped.

'Don't ever let anyone or anything keep you from believing in your dreams and from chasing them to make them come true. That's what I tell all the kids here. If I had given up on mine I would never have come off the streets.'

Jomi stared at her. Aunty Bisi had been a street kid? Wow, and then she'd made it to becoming a nurse and taking care of a whole bunch of kids.

'OK, Jomi? Hold on tight to your dreams and

hopes,' she said gently. She was waiting for him to say something.

Jomi's throat was so tight that he couldn't speak. But he nodded.

A loud chirping crescendo came down the tree.

Aunty Bisi looked up, her eyes confused.

Jomi smiled. Ghost was awake. The swishing of leaves told him she was jumping her way down. An almost silent thud followed, then the whisk of a bushy tail and she was beside him.

He held out the chunk of banana he'd saved for her.

'Oh, she is gorgeous,' Aunty Bisi said softly.

Jomi felt his chest warm up with pride. He was so relieved that Aunty Bisi liked her.

Ghost eyed Aunty Bisi warily at the sound of her voice. But after deciding she was OK, she snatched the banana out of his hand and stuffed it into her mouth in one smooth movement. With a sweep of her tail, she was back up in the tree.

'That . . .' Jomi said, 'was Ghost.'

# CHAPTER 19

# LAGOS LET'S DANCE

'L-L-D. L-L-D. L-L-D.'

The kids chanted the letters over and over again.

Jomi watched, his eyes darting from the kids to Aunty Bisi and back to Tanks and the others jumping around and singing. What was going on?

Aunty Bisi grinned. 'OK, OK, I'll get the laptop and you kids clear away the books in the meantime.'

Prosper and Chuks snatched up everyone's exercise books and put them in a pile. Tanks grabbed the duster and wiped off the exercises from the black wall. Jomi knew now why one wall in the living room was painted black.

Hassan came in from the bedroom, where he'd been all this while. He was the only one who hadn't taken part in the lessons. Hassan and Aunty Bisi didn't really seem to get on well at all. He was always frowning and disappearing in her presence.

But now he was grinning and looking just as excited as the others. What was LLD?

Aunty Bisi set up her laptop on a stool in front of the sofa.

'Good job, Jomi,' Aunty Bisi said. 'I liked how you helped Anna with her reading just now. How would you like to help her regularly? Every day a little bit of reading?'

Anna grinned at Jomi and he smiled back. 'Yes, I can do that.' The smile left his face when he saw Hassan scowling at him.

Prosper did a twirl and the others began the chant again.

'What's LLD?' Jomi asked.

Tanks gasped. 'You mean you don't know LLD?'

Jomi felt foolish.

'*LLD* is for *Lagos Let's Dance*, the best show in the world.' Her eyes were glowing with excitement.

Why did that sound strangely familiar? *Lagos*

*Let's Dance*. Where had he heard that before?

Prosper began doing the most amazing dance moves. The others formed a circle around him crying: 'Go Prosper, go Prosper!' That's when it hit him.

*Lagos Let's Dance*! The show his mum had mentioned in her letter. They were going to watch the show his mum loved watching. The screen of Aunty Bisi's laptop went on and the show began. Jomi's heart began thumping hard.

Two ladies in lovely dresses and a man in a fine suit were dancing their way on to a brightly lit stage and a huge audience cheered.

'A warm welcome to our wonderful judges,' the presenter cried. 'As usual I am your host Nneka Oji, and I am delighted to be here.'

Nneka Oji was the most beautiful woman Jomi had ever seen. He had to force himself to take his eyes off her and watch the judges she was introducing. Each of them spread out their arms on hearing their names, performed a quick dance move and twirled around before they sat on one of the three grand red velvet chairs at the side of the stage. The audience went wild and in the background the lights of the grand arena-like hall switched from a dim red to blue, then to a deep green, and then burst into a firework of colours.

There had to be almost a thousand people in that hall.

The others had already seated themselves by the time Jomi remembered where he was. He was the only one still standing. Aunty Bisi sat with the twins and Ivie on the lumpy sofa while the others were seated on the floor at their feet. Hassan was sitting at the table, away from the rest.

'Commot ya big head out of the way,' Hassan snapped when he caught Jomi glancing at him.

Jomi ducked his head and went to sit on the ground with Tanks and Prosper and Chuks.

'No pidgin English in here!' Aunty Bisi warned.

Jomi could feel Hassan's eyes boring sizzling holes through the back of his head, but he didn't care. He was going to watch the show that his mum loved.

He couldn't believe it. His mum was sitting somewhere out there in this very moment, just like him, excited to be watching the show. He could almost feel her in the empty space beside him, a soft smile on her face.

Dramatic opening music began and everyone around him hummed along. Jomi wished he also knew the melody. Then there was a countdown from ten to one and Jomi joined in yelling, 'Five, four, three, two, one.'

'Welcome back to another super-exciting episode of *Lagos Let's Dance*,' Nneka Oji said. She might as well have sprung out of a fairy tale. Her long silky green dress swayed softly around her body and looked like a green river held down by a golden belt.

The dancers she called first were wearing shiny red-and-black costumes. They pounced on to the stage like lions and began to do the most acrobatic and fantastic moves Jomi had ever seen. It was as if he'd been transported into another world. A world of beautiful people, talented people, some as young as he was and others so old they had grey hair and wrinkles in their faces. But all of them were connected by their love of music and rhythm and by their super-amazing dance moves.

The first groups of dancers finished and there

was a short break.

Jomi wanted the show to continue; he didn't want any break time.

Prosper jumped up and began doing a recap of the dance moves.

He grabbed his shorter leg and held it in the air and played it like a guitar just like one kid in the show had done.

'Na me sabi am pass,' Hassan cried, copying him. He was really good as well.

'Will you please speak correct English, Hassan? If you want to have a good job in future, you really should make some more effort. I know you can do better!' Aunty Bisi said. 'And besides that, as the oldest, I expect you to be a good example to the younger ones here.'

Hassan went rigid. He dropped his guitar leg and from one minute to the next the smile was gone from his eyes. He marched back to his stool and sat down with so much force that it creaked.

Aunty Bisi sighed. The air in the hot stuffy room felt even more stuffy as everyone glanced from Aunty Bisi to Hassan and back.

But then the *Lagos Let's Dance* melody came

back and Nneka Oji was smiling out of the screen. She had changed into a dazzling pink dress and pearl earrings. Everyone scrambled back to their seats. Hassan and Aunty Bisi's quarrel was forgotten. All that mattered, all that counted now was *Lagos Let's Dance*. The hot rhythms, the music making your insides tingle, the dance moves that made your eyes pop out of their sockets. Jomi's entire body vibrated with excitement and even worry for the dancers. He could feel the heat flow through his arms like the current through his wire cars when he connected them to the batteries. He already had a favourite team. He wanted the Danstars to win. He could hardly wait for the decision of the judges. Who would win and move up to the next round?

He pictured his mum somewhere in Lagos right now. Somewhere among the twenty million other people in this huge city. Was she thinking the same thing he was? Remembering that day when they'd danced beside the bus? How the passengers had clapped for her? Did she have her chin on her knees just like him as she remembered?

He glanced at the empty spot on the floor

beside him and could almost smell a tiny scent of ginger and lemon in the air. The squeezing longing in his chest was so painful. Did she really think he was angry with her? That he hadn't written on purpose?

He stretched out a hand to the space next to him.

## CHAPTER 20

# THE BREAKTHROUGH IDEA

'And we have a winner!' Nneka Oji cried. 'The Danstars have made it to the final round!'

The Danstars had done it. The team Jomi had been rooting for.

'Hurray!' Tanks cried and they high-fived each other.

'Danstars! Danstars!' they cried.

'Rubbish,' Hassan said. 'The others were better. The Danstars just had chubby baby faces – that's why they won.'

'No way,' Tanks cried. 'They won because they were the best.'

'Thank you so much as always for watching *LLD* and for being our biggest fans,' Nneka Oji said. 'And do not forget, if you have the dancing genes and the fire in your blood, then make sure to come to our auditions, taking place at the Lagos Let's Dance Plaza in Victoria Island. We will be preselecting the very best of the best dancers in Lagos for the next show.

'Everybody and anybody can take part in our free auditions. *Lagos Let's Dance* is waitiiiing . . .' She pointed a finger into the screen. 'For you.'

The screen went dark and the adverts came back on.

The words *everybody* and *anybody* and *free* echoed in Jomi's mind and an idea suddenly pushed its way through, jostling all other thoughts out of the way.

He sat up, his head suddenly a beehive of wildly buzzing and scattered thoughts.

It was too loud in here. He had to think. Tanks and Hassan were still arguing who the best team was and the others were dancing to the music that Aunty Bisi had put on. Jomi skirted through the tiny room, climbing over legs and pushing past dancing arms and out into the backyard. He was as out of breath as if he had just danced on the stage with the Danstars.

It was completely dark and the tree looked like

a giant with a huge afro being blown around by the night wind. He made to whistle a call but Ghost was already swishing down through the tree towards him.

'Hey,' he said when she hopped on his shoulder. 'Are you all right up there?'

She made a series of twittering noises in response and he knew she was fine. She was managing, just as he was. He could feel it in the warm gaze of her huge round eyes. And in her sticky paws and the intensely sweet scent of mango that hovered around her.

'You're having a ball up there, aren't you?' He laughed and watched her lick her paws.

'Do you think anything is possible?' he asked her softly.

She stopped her licking and looked up. In the ray of light that came from the house it was like gazing into an ocean. A warm, chocolaty ocean with swirls of soft sweetness. He felt strangely calm. She chirped and jumped off his shoulder in a grand leap. He twittered a similar sound and stared after her as she leapt from branch to branch. She was at the top within a minute.

He sighed. The tree was huge but it wasn't a forest. In the long run he would have to find a better solution for them. He leant his back against the tree's thick trunk. Ghost flitted up and down, jumping here and there while he tried to mould his idea into shape. The idea seemed almost too preposterous to think through. Could he be that bold?

'Jomi?'

Tanks stuck her head out into the yard.

Not surprisingly, Chuks and Prosper popped their heads out a second later and three shadows walked towards him.

'I just had a weird idea,' Jomi said, still feeling a bit overwhelmed by the magnitude of it. Would they think he was going over the top?

'I think I know how I can find my mum!' Speaking it out loud had him feeling more resolute. Even though his idea was forming itself out of strips and shreds of hope and fear, it was nevertheless taking shape. Like one of his toy cars built out of nothing but scrap.

*Nothing is impossible*, he thought, taking a deep breath.

'Tell us,' Tanks said.

'My mum . . .' Jomi gulped. 'My mum watches every single *LLD* show. She told me in her letter. So, I just had the idea, that all I need to do is be in one of the shows.'

The three shadows in front of him were very still. He could barely see their eyes but he could feel their stares, heavy on him.

'That is the most mind-blowing idea,' Tanks said.

'But, I don't get it,' Chuks said. 'How would you actually be in the show?'

'If I could audition and make it in,' Jomi said quietly.

'Wow, yes!' Prosper cried.

'Then she would see him and know he is in Lagos!' Tanks cried, putting her hands up to her cheeks. 'It is the craziest idea I have ever heard, but it could actually work. Nneka Oji said auditions are free and that anybody can come.'

Jomi smiled, relieved that they didn't think him completely stupid.

'All you need to do is make sure your face shows in the camera while you are dancing,'

Prosper said. 'Your mum would recognize you.'

'And then she would come to the LLD Plaza and you would be united,' Tanks said, hugging herself dramatically and swirling around. 'Oh my goodness, Jomi, that is the best idea ever!'

'Oh, but wait,' Chuks said. 'Can you even dance?'

Jomi's belly tightened at this. 'Well, I can, I mean . . . I'm not the best . . . but . . .'

'We could join you,' Prosper said. His shadow began fidgeting and wriggling about in the darkness. 'We could be a dance crew like the Danstars, with a cool choreography and costumes and then you would have better chances and you won't feel alone and shy.'

'W-would you help me?' Jomi felt relief and hope rush into his chest. He knew he could do some good moves but he couldn't actually imagine himself going up alone on a stage and doing a whole five-minute dance.

'Of course!' Tanks said. 'We could all practise, every day.' Her voice was high-pitched and almost breaking with excitement.

'If I don't need to do solo parts then I'm in,'

Chuks said.

'I don't mind solos,' Prosper said. He grabbed his leg and soon he was a bright-eyed shadow doing the guitar again.

'Oooh, this is so exciting,' Tanks said.

'What should we call our crew? We'll need to think of a super-cool name,' Prosper said.

'A pity Hassan is such a beast at the moment. He is actually the next best dancer after Prosper,' Tanks said.

'Do you think any of the others would want to join?' Jomi asked.

Chuks and Tanks shook their heads. 'Ivie always says she can't dance, Anna is too small and the twins would never dance in public. They are much too shy.'

'OK so we're four, unless Hassan wants to join, which I am not sure is even a good idea,' Jomi said. He didn't want Hassan spoiling things for him.

'Unfortunately, we'll need to ask him either way because he's the only one with a phone. He has the best jams on it.' Tanks fiddled with her plaits. 'If he doesn't agree to help us, then we have a problem because we won't have any music.'

## CHAPTER 21

## OBSTACLES

'Are you for real? You guys don kolo?' Hassan said, his voice a wicked sneer. 'Are you really so stupid to think you have a chance?'

No one replied.

They'd whispered about everything, making plans and worrying about how to ask Hassan all yesterday evening and all morning. And now finally when they'd mustered up the courage to come out to the backyard to ask him, he'd reacted exactly the way they'd hoped he wouldn't. And secretly known he would.

Even worse, Hassan began to laugh, a harsh, snorty laugh that cut to the bone. Jomi shrank into his skin. His idea suddenly seemed immensely stupid and outrageous.

Ivie pushed between Hassan and Tanks and

began to make really quick signs.

'This is not about me being mean,' Hassan hissed. 'This is about them having the most foolish and kolo idea of all time.'

'Well, you don't need to join our crew then,' Tanks said. 'All we need from you is to allow us use your phone.'

'Oh, so you actually thought I would join your club of losers?' Hassan cried, his eyes widening in mock shock. He laughed again.

'Let's go,' Tanks said. 'Waste of time.'

'Wetin una wan do with my phone?' Hassan called after them.

'We need music to practise our dance,' Prosper said.

'And why the hell should I lend you my phone?'

No one replied.

'Were you planning on sharing the fifty million Naira win with me?' This time he laughed so hard he fell off the bench.

'You are such an idiot, Hassan,' Tanks cried. 'Why do you always have to spoil everything?'

Hassan's face turned serious. For a brief moment he looked almost hurt.

'You suppose dey grateful that I'm telling you the truth before you disgrace yourselves on national TV. You don't even stand the slightest chance against all those fine-fine rich people pikin. I mean, look at you! Omo, dem go finish una for there!'

'We know that the idea is a little bit . . . big,' Jomi said.

Hassan snorted.

Jomi could hardly look at Hassan while he spoke. Hassan had disliked him from the first moment they'd met. And Jomi didn't like him either. But he needed to swallow his pride and do this to find his mum.

'It's not like we think we'll win. That's not even our plan. We just want to make it as far as the first rounds.'

'And what's the point of that?' Hassan leant into the tree trunk, obviously enjoying his superior position. It was difficult to watch him so full of himself. *Like a stupid king of a mango tree*, Jomi thought, crunching his fingers into fists. Hot angry waves were beginning to rush through his insides.

'Jomi's mum watches *LLD*,' Tanks explained. 'She doesn't miss an episode. The plan is, she would see him and come and get him and they would be reunited.'

'Aww my heart wan melt, sooo touching,' Hassan said and began making smooshy kissing noises.

'I thought you would be happy about the part where you could get rid of me.' The words burst out of Jomi, surprising him. 'Isn't that what you've wanted since the moment you met me?'

Hassan watched him for a moment, his face not showing any emotion. Then he folded his arms across his chest. 'Nothing comes free in this life. If you wan borrow my phone you will pay. Fifty naira per session.'

'What?' Tanks cried. 'Where are we to get that kind of money from?'

Hassan picked up his phone, punched in something and there was a dialling tone.

'My guy,' he said, 'wetin dey happen? Abeg come save me from here, I dey very bored today.'

Jomi trudged back into the house with the others. His legs felt heavy. Would the others give up? He still wanted to do it. They just needed to find other ways of getting music to practise. But he couldn't do this alone. He hoped they weren't too put off by Hassan.

'Who says we are not planning to win?' Prosper said the minute they were inside. 'If I'm going to take part, I'm definitely going there to win.' He began rippling his body into a series of hot moves.

They all burst into giggles.

'We're definitely not letting that one stop us,' Tanks said. 'We'll find another way.'

'Thank you,' Jomi said.

'For what?' Tanks said. 'We are in this together, don't worry. We will do everything possible to get you into *LLD*.'

Goosebumps formed on Jomi's arms and his eyes felt wet.

'We have to find a way to make some cool costumes though,' Chuks said.

'Maybe Ivie can help us, get some cheap material to sew something,' Tanks said. 'We'll have to be creative because we can't buy any cool costumes.'

'And, we'll have to save money for the bus fare to Victoria Island also,' Jomi added.

They all nodded.

'There's quite a lot of money involved though,' Prosper said quietly.

Something heavy filled the air around them like a cold gust of harmattan wind.

'Being poor always makes things so much harder, doesn't it?' Tanks said.

'That's why we'll just have to win and get the fifty million naira prize!' Chuks said.

Everyone began talking and giggling and dancing all at the same time. The excitement was infectious.

Jomi sat in a corner and watched them all making plans, and his heart warmed. They all wanted to help him be with his mum.

Tanks joined him in his corner and together they watched Prosper and Chuks practise some dance moves. Tanks pulled out her little notebook. She scribbled something into it.

'A new special thing for your list?' he asked.

She grinned. 'I just joined a dance crew that's going to audition for *Lagos Let's Dance*. Things have been getting exciting around here since you came, Jomi. I think you may be special.'

Jomi felt awkward. He definitely didn't feel special. The only other person who had ever told him he was special was his mum. But she'd left him, hadn't she?

What if this all failed? What if he didn't ever find his mum? What if there was nothing special about him?

He jumped up. 'Do you have a scrapyard or a scrap shop around here?' His fingers were itching. They were practically burning to find some scrap, anything that someone had thrown away. He would make something useful out of it.

And he had one particular piece of scrap in mind.

A broken radio.

## CHAPTER 22

# OVERCOMING OBSTACLES

There was no scrapyard around that anyone knew of. But there was a magic place called E-corner. It had rows and rows of electronic repairs shops, so amazing that Jomi staggered starry-eyed through the rows, not getting enough of the sights. How could this even be real?

Little cabins side by side, tightly packed, shelves bulging with every single electronic gadget or spare part he could imagine. It was like an electronic paradise and if they hadn't had other more important plans, Jomi would have spent the entire day gawking at the shop owners as they turned tiny screws into the backs of phones, clipped wires, fixed hard plastic covers with superglue and cut through thin metal with miniature saws.

Jomi sighed. He knew exactly what job he wanted to do when he was grown up. If he could own a shop like this and fix things all day, he knew he would be the happiest person that ever lived.

This was a quieter place than the market. Not as rowdy and busy. Faint music played from one cabin and some heads bobbed along with the rhythm.

'Which one should we ask?' Chuks whispered.

'They all look so busy,' Tanks said. They were walking through rows a second time now.

'Let's ask here,' Jomi said, approaching an older-looking man.

'Good morning sir, do you have a music player?'

The bushy white cloud of hair that had been hovering intently over a working table bobbed up to reveal an old face and a pair of thick-rimmed glasses.

Blurry eyes peered through the glasses, which were held together at the middle with black sticky tape.

The man dropped a pair of tweezers on the table, wiped the sweat off his forehead and took a swig of water.

Then he eyed them all one by one, taking in three boys and a girl, dusty feet in old flip-flops and rough sandals.

'I can't dash you o,' he said. 'You get money?'

The others fidgeted nervously but Jomi wasn't worried. This man was a collector like him. His shop was brimming with thousands of old gadgets, cables, wires and spare parts. The parts on the upper shelves were covered with layers of dust as thick as icing on a cake. This man had so many things he hadn't even used or touched for months.

Jomi heaved his rucksack off his back and groped around inside it.

'We don't have money but we can exchange things.' He spread out his coil of fresh copper wire, his good pliers and his solar-powered torch on the old man's working table. The man peered down at the things and his eyes lit up at the solar-powered torch.

'Dis one dey work?' he asked, pointing at it.

Jomi nodded. 'But you have to leave it out in the sun for a while.'

'I know,' the man mumbled. He examined the

torch briefly and then got up. He began searching around in the huge cartons behind him.

Chuks and Prosper grinned at Jomi but Tanks made a sign to them to be quiet.

'Ah, I don see am,' the man said, pulling out a curious black box.

He dropped it on the table and they stared at it.

'Ahn-ahn, but this is a cassette player,' Jomi said. Disappointment filled his belly, making it feel heavy like after eating old beans.

'Na only this I get for you,' the man replied. 'It even get cassette for inside,' he added. He clicked it open and pulled out an old cassette titled '*80s mixtape*'. He held it up as if it were a gold nugget.

'Does it work?'

'Radio don spoil but cassette player is very good.'

Jomi sighed. This ancient cassette player would have to do.

There was no electricity as usual when they got back, but Jomi found four batteries that still worked in his rucksack and they soon had the cassette player running.

The mixtape was useless. Music from the 1980s filled the living room and they stared at each other disappointed. Fela and Sunny Ade were fine for listening but definitely not for the kind of dance moves they needed.

'Mehn, we want to dance at *LLD*, not at a grandpa's ninetieth birthday party. They'll boo us off stage with this kind of old-school stuff,' Prosper muttered. 'We need the good stuff with the hot beats. We need gwara-gwara and shaku-shaku.'

'Yeah, we want to dance umlando and legwork,' Chuks added, throwing a glance at Jomi.

Jomi took the cassette player outside and sat on the bench under the mango tree. The heat indoors was unbearable.

The others watched him unscrew the back of the player and take off the casing.

He held it out to Prosper who took it carefully.

'And you really know what you are doing?' Prosper didn't sound very convinced.

Jomi nodded, clamping the screw between his teeth and glancing at the insides. He'd done things like this hundreds of times before. That was the advantage of living close to a scrap hill. He'd had hundreds of broken stuff to practise and experiment on. He'd soon gotten the hang of electric circuits, the flow of current, transistors and capacitors which were often broken. His science teacher at school had told him the names of the parts long after he'd already known what they did and how to fix them.

He could already spot what was wrong with the radio in a minute and was soon rummaging around in his pockets.

Tanks hadn't said much since they came back. He glanced at her.

'You know this doesn't help us with practising choreos, right?'

He nodded.

'We need to be able to replay our songs again and again to practise a choreography. Having the radio running won't do it.'

'I know, but this is where the cassette player comes in handy. You'll see.'

'Hope you have it running soon,' Prosper said. 'We need to hear music to get some inspiration.

We need ideas for choreography.' He started shuffling Happy Feet steps across the backyard, sliding sideways like a cute lopsided robot.

'Yeah, we need to be unique and different,' Tanks said. 'We can't just copy any choreos we've seen and re-use them. Remember what the judges always say, if there isn't anything special about the dance you don't stand a chance.'

'Yeah, anybody can dance a simple shaku-shaku, nothing special about that,' Prosper said.

'Are you guys really sure we can do this at all?' Chuks asked.

'Chuks, don't kill our vibe before we even get started,' Tanks snapped. 'We are going to do this.'

Jomi screwed the casing back on and they watched him in silence. He twisted the tuning knob and soon rumbling radio voices sailed out of the radio.

'Yay,' Prosper cried. 'You're the man!' He high-fived Jomi.

Jomi found a music station but the music wasn't much better than on the tape.

'Goodness, if we have to wait for hours every day until a song worth dancing to comes, we'll never get a choreography together,' Tanks said.

'How about the other side of the tape?' Prosper asked.

'It's an eighties tape. It's only going to play eighties music,' Jomi replied but he flipped the cassette and pressed play.

Just in that moment, Hassan came out to the backyard. He was followed by a girl and two other boys, as tall as he was.

Hadn't Aunty Bisi said no visitors?

'Look at these losers,' Hassan said the moment he caught sight of them. He spread his arms. 'My friends, may I introduce the dance crew who think they will be the next *LLD* champions.'

'For real?' the girl asked, looking interested, but the other boys eyed them and sniggered.

'Listen to that ancient music from that piece of junk.'

Jomi felt a hot, fuzzy ball of something forming in his chest. The same angry ball he felt any time he walked over scrap hills and found the most amazing things that had been thrown away as if they were nothing. He wouldn't allow his new cassette player to be declared useless.

Even though Hassan and his friends loomed tall and many around them, Jomi couldn't stop himself.

'Just because something isn't new or shiny, doesn't make it junk,' he hissed.

'This,' Hassan said, raising his foot to jab at the music player, 'is definitely a piece of rubbish.'

'Hassan! Stop!' Tanks cried, rushing forward. But it was too late and the player fell off the bench, with a loud crash.

'What is wrong with you?' Tanks cried. She poked his chest, but he pushed her away with such force that she staggered backwards and fell to the ground.

Prosper and Jomi helped her up and Chuks knelt down beside the recorder, checking to see if it was broken.

'Don't worry,' Jomi said. 'It's not broken. It's tough and robust. And even if it breaks, I'll find a way to fix it.'

'You can't make something cool out of rubbish. And that's why your dance crew has no chance at *LLD*,' Hassan sneered. Then he nodded to the other corner of the yard. 'Make we go that side,' he said to his friends. He brought out his phone and music beats began to pour out of his playlist.

'So that old-model phone with its cracked screen is what makes you better than us?' Jomi snapped.

A snort burst out of one of Hassan's friends and the other two grinned.

Hassan slithered to a stop like a very angry python.

Jomi took a small step backwards. Had he gone too far? What had made him say that?

The venomous look that Hassan gave him before moving on made his insides wobble. Why did he have the feeling that he had just made Hassan into an even bigger enemy?

## CHAPTER 23

# A DANCE CREW NEEDS A NAME

Hassan and his friends connected his phone to a loudspeaker they'd brought along and began dancing. They were good.

'I can't believe they would just steal our idea of going to audition for *LLD*,' Chuks whispered.

'Do you think that's what they're up to?' Jomi asked, glancing sideways at them, so they wouldn't notice him staring. He still felt shaky from Hassan's wicked glare.

'It seems obvious,' Tanks said. 'But we don't need to care about them. We'll be better.'

'Remember, all we want to do is get in, so Jomi's mum can see him,' Chuks said. 'This is not about being better or worse than them.'

'Yes,' Prosper said. 'And also remember what

the judges said. Not necessarily the best dancers win anyway. It's all about originality.'

Jomi glanced at Hassan and his friends. Their moves were sleek and cool. Hassan knew all the latest dance steps and he and his friends had the best music to practise with. At the moment, all his crew had was an ancient music player and an outdated cassette.

Jomi examined the music player. It had a scratch on the side where it had hit the ground but the old thing was strong and had survived the crash just like he'd known it would. Old gadgets were much more solid.

'So, what should we do now?' Tanks asked. 'We can't practise here with these ones around. Or should we just dance along to their music?'

Jomi was just cleaning the button with the red letters 'rec'.

'I have an idea,' he said, putting his finger to his lips with a grin.

He pressed the 'rec' button and made a sign for them to follow him back inside.

'What did you do? What was your idea?'

Jomi threw himself on to one of the mattresses

on the floor of the bedroom. It was stuffy and hot but at least they had privacy.

'What's that red button you pressed?' Chuks asked.

'It's for recording,' Jomi grinned. 'While Hassan and his friends practise, we'll just record all their music and then we'll have their playlist to choose songs from and practise moves on.'

'Na wa o!' Tanks cried. 'That's brilliant.'

'They think they're better but we'll show them that we are not rubbish,' Jomi said.

'Imagine beating them with their own music,' Prosper giggled.

'Best thing ever,' Tanks said and high-fived him.

'All we need now is an original idea,' Prosper said.

Prosper was right. They really had to think about what the judges had said.

'There's nothing unique about what Hassan was doing,' Prosper went on. 'They were just dancing the same old dances that everyone knows from the videos. We need new choreography.'

'Yeah, you're right,' Tanks said.

'We have to invent our own fantastic choreography. A choreo that tells a story. Our own special story.'

The room fell silent. Jomi could practically hear the brain cells of the others working hard, like pistons trying to get a motor going. His own brain kept going around in circles but not coming up with any ideas. It was like trying to get a car out of a deep pothole, the tyres rotating wildly and the car not moving an inch.

Prosper got up after a while and began to shuffle around. Tanks joined him but they soon gave up.

'It's no use. We need a motto or an idea first, then we can create the dance for it.'

'How about our crew name?' Jomi asked. 'Maybe that could help. If we find a name that fits us. Then maybe we'll know what we stand for and what kind of dance fits us?'

'Yes,' Tanks cried. 'What is important to us? What do we stand for?' She clapped her hands and stared at them bright-eyed. Jomi sat up and Chuks and Prosper also looked at her eagerly.

'Me, I'm fearless,' Tanks said, pounding her chest.

'Yeah, we know,' Chuks said with a grin.

'The only thing I have ever been afraid of in my life is hunger. And that's only because hunger is sneaky and creeps into your belly when you're not careful and not watching out. If it would stand up and face me I would fight it.' She made a grim face and boxed the air in front of her.

Jomi giggled. He could definitely imagine Tanks giving a thin, scrawny monster called Hunger a left hook under the chin.

'Me, I'm a survivor,' Prosper said. 'Nothing can bring me down.'

'Yeah,' Tanks said, and gave Prosper a fist bump. She started singing, '*I'm a survivor, I ain't gon give up, I'm a survivor, keep on surviving.*'

'I know that song,' Jomi said.

'Yeah, it's from Destiny's Child.'

'Do you all believe in destiny?' Jomi glanced up, eager to hear what they would say.

'You mean like our destinies being carved in stone and all that?' Tanks shook her head. 'I'm writing my own destiny. Not letting anyone decide my future for me.'

'But I heard people say that we chose our

destinies before we were born and that we can't ever change them,' Prosper said. 'Though that doesn't make sense to me. Why would I have chosen my life the way it is?' He looked at Jomi as if he was expecting an answer, but Jomi didn't have one.

'My dad always used to say everything has a reason,' Chuks said. 'That God planned our destinies for us and we have to trust him because he knows best. Even when my dad was ill and knew he would soon die, he said it was all for a reason and that everything would eventually turn out for the best. He said maybe all the bad things that happened to us were meant to make me grow up tough so I could one day do great things.' Chuks bit his lip and looked away out of the window. 'I'd rather have a dad than grow up tough to do great things one day.'

'My mum said sometimes your destiny takes a while to start working,' said Jomi, 'because destinies are sometimes lazy and sleeping. She said sometimes you need to force your destiny to finally wake up and do what she was meant to do.'

'And how are we meant to force our destinies to start working?' Tanks asked.

'By taking the first steps, working hard, dreaming big, I guess.'

'Well, we're definitely dreaming big at the moment,' Prosper said. 'We dreaming of going to dance on the biggest stage in Lagos.'

'Yeah, we pushing our destinies,' Chuks said, and did some air boxing too.

'All four of us have our own separate destinies but isn't it funny how all our destinies brought us together, here in this room right now?' Tanks said. 'Isn't that a strange feeling? For some reason the four of us are all sitting here and planning something big. Maybe it's just a coincidence that all our destinies cross here, but what if it is the beginning of something special?'

'What if we call ourselves Destiny's Children?' Jomi asked.

'Wooah, yes,' Tanks said, jumping up. 'Or Destiny's Crew.'

'Even better,' Jomi said.

'That is sooo cool,' Prosper said. 'We gonna hammaa!'

Chuks gave a thumbs up.

Jomi's legs were all tingly and he could feel the excitement of the others as well. Sweet, swavy beats floated into the bedroom from Hassan's phone at the back and they began to dance.

'OK, so we have a name. Now, what is our story?' Jomi asked.

Prosper said, 'The judges always ask: "What is special about your crew? What do you want to show with your dance? Why do you think you are better than your rivals?"'

'We are tough,' Tanks cried.

'We are survivors,' Prosper said with a grin.

'We are going to do great things,' Chuks added, pumping and flexing his arm muscles.

'We are not rubbish,' Jomi yelled, loud enough for Hassan and his friends to hear.

## CHAPTER 24

# DREAMERS

'Good morning my lovelies!' Aunty Bisi's voice was like being woken by your favourite song playing on the radio.

She was smiling in through the door, looking bright in an orange dress and a white hairband. Heads bobbed up from mattresses around Jomi as he rubbed his eyes.

'There's steaming-hot akara and bread on the table for everyone. I'll be running the shop for Landlord today and we'll do our lessons afterwards, OK?'

Aunty Bisi's head popped away. 'Anna, you can come over when you're ready,' she called on her way back out.

'Is today different?' Jomi asked Prosper, whose mattress he now shared.

'Yep,' Prosper said. 'Saturdays are different. Aunty Bisi works in the shop in front on Saturdays because that's Landlord's free day. One of us gets to spend the day with her in the shop. This week is Anna's turn.'

Jomi hurried out into the backyard to check on Ghost before she slept. With a few quick movements he was up in the tree and climbing his way towards the nest they'd created for her.

'Hello Ghost,' he whispered and carefully slipped his hand into the gourd.

She nuzzled his hand but was obviously already too tired to come out. So, he just sat there for a while thinking about his mum, *LLD* and their dance moves – which they still had to work on.

Then he plucked a few mangoes and hurried down. He should go get his share of breakfast before it was all gone.

Jomi could feel an underlying buzz of excitement in the air. It was always like that when Aunty Bisi was here.

Chuks and Prosper were doing an extra round of cleaning the bathroom and Tanks was arranging the bedroom and singing. Only Hassan was still lying on his mattress and fiddling with his phone which was charging.

Even though he didn't know Aunty Bisi that well yet, Jomi's belly fluttered about at the thought of spending the evening with her.

'Do you guys think we should have another go at selling mangoes?' Tanks asked when they sat down for breakfast. She was stuffing her juicy akara into her mouth but her eyes were on the mangoes he'd plucked off the tree. 'They look really good. Perfect ripeness to sell. We really need to start saving up money for the bus fare to Victoria Island for *LLD*.'

Jomi sighed. Their round of mango selling in traffic hadn't brought in anything even worth mentioning. How were they ever going to get enough money for the bus journey? If only there was a scrapyard close by. He could have fixed things and tried to sell them to that repairman in his shop. He should go back and try to sell his copper wire. That might bring in something. Why hadn't he done that last time?

'Pity we can't just ask Aunty Bisi for the money,' Chuks said.

Prosper and Tanks stared at him, all silent, contemplating the idea. From what Jomi knew of grown-ups, they were always so negative about the best and most fun ideas. Telling her about *LLD* was probably not a good idea.

Tanks shook her head. 'She doesn't even have any money. The other day I heard her whispering on the phone with a friend. Aunty Bisi said her husband is angry with her. He wants them to move out of his brother's house where they're staying now. He is angry that all her salary goes into the rent for this place and they don't have enough for their own place.'

Jomi felt a chill go down his spine. That didn't sound good. Chuks and Prosper didn't look happy either.

'She wouldn't even take us seriously, anyway,' Tanks said quietly. 'Adults never do.'

Prosper grabbed three of the mangoes. 'Yeah, she would never let us go all the way to Victoria Island on our own. She'll say it's too dangerous.' He began to juggle the mangoes.

Chuks snatched one away mid-air and the others toppled on to the table.

Jomi giggled as they grappled with the mangoes and punched each other playfully. One mango thudded on to the ground.

Tanks rolled her eyes. 'You'll ruin them.'

'No point trying to sell them anyway,' Chuks said. 'We need to get money another way.'

'If only we had something more exciting to sell than mangoes,' Prosper said, his face serious again.

Anna appeared in the doorway. She was holding a plastic bag in one hand and her doll was pressed tightly to her chest with the other.

'Aunty Bisi sends plantain chips for everyone,' she called, dropping the plastic bag on the table.

'Did you cry, Anna?' Tanks asked, pulling her into a hug and wiping her face.

'A lady wanted to buy my doll for her baby,' Anna said. 'She thought it was for buying and selling because I left her lying on the counter. Her baby was crying and didn't want to give it back. But Aunty Bisi didn't allow it! The woman's baby had to give it back. She is mine!' She cradled the doll tightly.

'Yeah, way to go Anna,' Prosper said. 'Fight for your right!'

Anna grinned. 'Bye,' she called and ran back around the house to the front shop. Her footsteps pitter-pattered away.

Hassan came out of the bedroom and immediately jostled Chuks for the bag with the plantain chips. His phone, which was sticking out of his shorts pocket, was playing loud music.

'Ouch,' Chuks cried and sat back down, rubbing his arm.

'Stupid dreamers,' Hassan said and disappeared back into the bedroom with his plantain chips.

'I'd rather be a dreamer than a pretender,' Tanks hissed after him.

Hassan's head popped back through the door. 'What do you mean by pretender?'

'We saw you practising with your friends yesterday. Don't think we don't know you are also planning to audition for *LLD*.'

Hassan began to laugh his nasty laugh. 'Don't worry, you don't need to fear getting beaten by us. We go leave the *LLD* plans to dreamers like you. We are planning something bigger.'

'Yeah right,' Tanks mumbled.

'We're going viral if you need to know.'

'What's viral?' Prosper asked.

'It means we'll be famous on Instagram and YouTube. I got accounts on social media.' He held up his phone and grinned. 'Something you dreamers can only dream about. And anyway, we're going to be uploading our dance videos. We gonna be so famous and I no mean like any Lagos type of famous or Nigeria type of famous, I mean worldwide type of freaking famous.'

Hassan wriggled his eyebrows and disappeared back into the bedroom.

They stared at each other.

Jomi shrugged.

'All we want to do is get into the show,' Tanks said.

Her voice was quiet and somehow, she didn't sound like that was all they wanted to do. Now that they had a real plan and a crew name, it felt like they wanted to try and win as well.

Jomi imagined himself on stage with the others and Nneka Oji, saying: *And the winner is Destiny's Crew!* And handing them the trophy. His heart thumped faster at the thought of his mum seeing this on TV.

She would be so proud of him. If he could just make her look at him in that special way she used to. He could still remember the look, even though the memory had blurred and it always felt like he was looking back in time through cracked binoculars.

If he could make her see he was worth it.

He closed his eyes and tried to remember her voice. *Do you know why I gave you your name, Jomi? Because you were my very first surprise in life. My very own special surprise.*

His heart suddenly felt like it didn't have enough space in his chest. Like his chest was too tight and he couldn't breathe. He jumped up, pushing the chair backwards abruptly. He had to stop being a dreamer. If he wanted to find his mum, he would have to be serious about things.

'Let's go practise. We need a choreo and we need a really good story.'

# CHAPTER 25

# INVENTING DANCE MOVES

'Jomi, you haven't seen my backflip yet, have you?'

Chuks waved a broken clothes hanger around while he spoke, holding it like a flag. He'd been fiddling around with it while they'd cracked their heads about dance moves and how to choreograph their steps.

'Oya, watch this,' he said and leant his lanky figure backwards, hands over his head. He reached for the floor behind him. The others moved away from him as he flipped over. Last minute, he remembered the clothes hanger he was still holding and flung it away. Then he toppled into a heap of tangled arms and legs and crashed into the wall.

'Chuks, I wonder if you ever noticed that our

backyard is not a football field?' Prosper said. 'Sorry to disappoint you but in reality, it's a tiny yard behind a tiny house. You have to look around and calculate space before you do backflips.'

'Yeah, so funny,' Chuks mumbled, rubbing his elbow.

'If you want us to include your backflip into our choreo, you may have to work on it a bit,' Tanks said.

Jomi scrambled after the clothes hanger which had landed beneath one of the benches. 'Nothing is ever useless,' he mumbled. His usual mantra on his scrap hill.

He was twisting the hanger into shape when the idea came. It hit him so suddenly that he stumbled and fell on to the bench with the force of it.

'I've got it,' he cried, holding the hanger up like a trophy.

'What, the hanger? Good for you, you are a hero Jomi,' Prosper said.

'I don't mean the hanger.' Jomi rolled his eyes. 'I just got an idea for our dance. What if our story is about us refusing to be called useless?'

'Heh? I don't understand,' Tanks said.

'Look at this broken clothes hanger here. Anybody would throw this away, right?' He held it up. 'But it would be perfect as an antenna for our radio. People always say things are rubbish and throw them away even though they might still be useful. They don't appreciate things any more as soon as they're not new. People are wasteful and always want newer and shinier things and don't care about the old ones any more.'

'I still don't get it?' Prosper said.

Jomi scratched his head, looking for words to explain. 'Like . . . what if our dance is about making the best of things, about fixing things, about not writing things off the minute they aren't perfect. We can show people that even if we are not dressed as fine and shiny as others, it doesn't mean we are useless.'

'Yeah, I think I get you,' Tanks said. 'Like we are strong and we can do great things even if our destinies have not been looking so good. Because we are survivors.'

'Yes,' Jomi cried.

Tanks shook her head. 'But how do we show that in a dance?'

'Well, we'll still have to think about making dance moves out of the idea.' Jomi's insides were practically roasting with the heat of the excitement inside him. He wished he could explain what he meant better.

'You know how some of our traditional dances tell stories. Like in school we had this Atilogwu dance group and their dances told the story of the farmer who went to the farm. One dance showed him sharpening his machete, another dance showed him cutting grass and another dance showed him flinging the grass away over his shoulder.'

Now they were nodding, so Jomi began to feel bolder. 'OK, so what if for example we start with a dance called . . .' He thought briefly. 'Thro'way.' He pressed the play button on their music player and it began to play the songs they'd recorded from Hassan's practice the day before.

Chuks and Prosper grinned as the music began to play.

Jomi listened for the rhythm of the song and then joined it. He leant forward and began dancing legwork steps while whirling the clothes hanger around. Then he flung the hanger on to the floor while twisting his legs in Awilo style. He hoped he'd looked swaggy and cool while throwing it, since it was meant to have looked like a dance move.

'Something like that?' he asked, looking up and suddenly feeling foolish. 'I guess, that didn't look very professional yet . . .'

'But it did!' Tanks clapped her hands. 'It did.'

She jumped forward. 'OK, I'm doing the next one. This next dance is called "Pick up".' She began to twist her waist slowly, bobbing her bum umlando-style like the girls in *LLD*.

Jomi's eyes almost plopped out of his head. He didn't know Tanks could dance like that.

Tanks grinned and with surprising ease and elegance, she twisted down slowly and picked up the hanger.

'Yaayy!!' They all cheered her.

'Now comes "Fix'am",' Chuks cried. He jumped forward, took the hanger from Tanks and began to move one hand just like in shaku-shaku and it looked as if he were fixing something. It was the perfect dance for Chuks because he usually looked rather jerky while dancing and this Fix'am dance was perfect for jerky moves. It was sooo good.

'Fix'am! Fix'am! Fix'am!' they called, clapping and chanting in rhythm.

'Now me!' Prosper cried. 'Mine is "Shine'am".'

He began to rub his hands over his head in rhythm, then over his face and body, like he was shining himself up with body cream. And the whole while he was dancing Happy Feet and sliding and popping his feet left and right. He was hilarious.

'You are so smoooooth!' Chuks called.

'We have it!' Tanks cried. She was so excited she was hopping around like when you forget your flip-flops and run out on the street at midday, burning your feet.

Jomi grinned. He felt exactly the same way.

## CHAPTER 26

# NIGHT NOISES

Jomi jumped up with a start. His pillow was soaked with sweat and it made a disgusting squishy noise as he moved. He turned it over.

The air was so thick with moisture, he could wave his hand through it a couple of times and have a handful of water. The nine of them breathing hot air into the tiny room was not helping.

The window was open but the curtain hung beside it like a heavy, damp sack, not even fluttering a tiny bit. No wind, no fresh air at all.

He wished he were still asleep. But something had woken him up. He remembered a loud, piercing sound.

There was a rustling and someone came over. The dark shape looked like Ivie.

She tapped his arm.

'I'm awake,' he whispered.

She began gesticulating fast, but it was too dark to see her hands and he had only learnt a few of her words so far.

What did she want?

Then he felt her hand tap his ear lightly. She wanted him to listen.

'Yes, I also thought I'd heard something.'

Suddenly a petrifying, heart-rending wail came from outside. A baby? A very sad baby?

Was a neighbour's baby crying? He rubbed his eyes and sat up properly. The cry came again.

It wasn't a baby. It was Ghost!

A gasp and fearful whimpering came from across the room. Anna.

'Shhh!' someone said. Ivie went over to her and rubbed her back.

Jomi groped his way about the tiny room, which was not easy with so many mattresses side by side. He stumbled over a leg.

'Chai,' the leg owner groaned. Sounded like Chuks, but it was too dark to see.

Powdery moonlight sprinkled into their living room as he drew open the curtains. He peered out into a foggy mush of greyness. The full moon was still trying to make an impression in the sky but not quite succeeding any more. It would soon be morning and the moon was blurring.

Was Ghost afraid? Or lonely?

He clicked open the back door and walked out. The mango tree felt even larger than usual, its presence dominating the yard. Another sad cry. Instinctively, Jomi raised his hands to his ears. It was so loud. Abruptly, the wail muffled into a twitter of little noises. Jomi heard her slashing through the leaves and branches. She was coming down. A squeaky cry, a flutter of leaves above him and then she was on his shoulders, her bushy tail sweeping his arm.

'Hey, Ghost,' he said. 'What's wrong?'

Her little limbs were trembling and she kept marching about on his shoulder, twisting in a circle. She couldn't sit still.

What did it mean?

'Are you worried? Afraid? Sad?' He stroked her back with his palm, down to her long tail, which swished this way and that. Again and again. Then he walked slowly around the tree, rubbing her back and mumbling calming words.

It seemed to be working. She nestled into his neck and stopped turning, her tail now still.

'Is it the moon?' he asked. Some animals reacted to full moons. Maybe she was excited about the moon? Or worried that it was fading?

He sat down on one of the benches and leant against the tree trunk. Ghost's steady breathing and warm body against his neck was soothing. Soon his eyelids felt like two heavy blankets, tucking his eyes away into a warm comfy sleep.

A shrill cry had him leaping off the bench. It was bright, early morning now and the first sunrays were penetrating the few gaps in the mango tree's crown.

Ghost was up in the tree screeching and wailing again. Her cry was almost unbearably sad.

'Hey Ghost! What is it? Don't you want to come down?'

But she didn't come.

The door to the house opened and the others peered out, rubbing their eyes.

'What is wrong with Ghost?' Anna asked.

'She's trying to drive us mad,' Hassan's voice

called. 'That's what bushbabies do. They cry outside people's windows at night until they run mad.'

Anna's face crumbled into a mess of tears and wobbly lips. She stared at the treetop, her eyes wide with fear, and slipped back inside behind the others.

Jomi peered up through the leaves. He couldn't bear the sad cries any more. He grabbed the rope and began to heave himself up.

Tanks, Prosper and Chuks were with him a second later, helping him up. Their faces were a mix of worry and fear.

'What is all that noise, this early in the morning?' an angry grown-up voice called from somewhere.

'Abeg, stop that noise,' another voice called.

Jomi climbed faster. A branch snapped and he grabbed hold of another to steady himself.

'Careful,' Tanks called from below.

Ghost wasn't in her nest. The cries were coming from the very top of the tree. Jomi went as far as he could. As far as the branches, which were now thinner and more brittle at the top, could carry him. Then he stopped.

'Ghost!' he called.

He waited, but she didn't come.

At least she'd stopped the crying.

He made a couple more twittering calls. He tried all the ones he'd learnt from Uncle Babatunde. But she didn't come. He couldn't see her. He just knew she was up there somewhere, listening to him but ignoring him. He wished with all his heart that he could help her.

If he only knew what was wrong.

## CHAPTER 27

# MORE PROBLEMS

'Is everyone OK? Anna, Ivie? Where is everyone?' What was Aunty Bisi doing here so late? It had to be past midnight already. She sounded so anxious.

Jomi hurried out of the bedroom behind Keni who was holding the candle. The others crowded out into the dark living room as well. There was a power failure again and Aunty Bisi was holding a torch which she pointed up at the ceiling to light up the room.

She looked different. Even though the room was only dimly lit, Jomi could see she wasn't her usual self. Her hair was bundled up under a hair-net and she was wearing a big T-shirt that was too large for her over a pair of shorts. She looked very, very tired.

After she'd counted them and made sure they were complete, the worried look changed into a frown.

'What is this I'm hearing about children screaming at night? I was already in bed when Landlord called me to say the neighbours had complained about last night.'

No one replied but uneasy glances shot in Jomi's direction.

'Jomi? What is it?' Aunty Bisi asked when she noticed their looks. 'Do you know anything about this? Were you playing outside at night?'

She looked back at the others. 'Didn't you all tell him the rules about being quiet at night and not drawing any attention to us? We can't get into any trouble here. If we get thrown out of here then that's the end of . . .'

Anna began to cry and Aunty Bisi placed an arm around her.

'It wasn't us,' Hassan said. 'It was that stupid, dirty animal of his. It's peeing all over the tree and its droppings are everywhere on our benches in the mornings. And now it has started screeching around at night.'

'I cleaned the droppings away already,' Jomi said quickly.

'The bushbaby?' Aunty Bisi's frown deepened.

'Hassan said we are all going to go mad soon because that's what bushbabies do. They drive people mad.' Anna was trembling all over. 'They cry under your window every night until you can't think straight any more.'

'What rubbish.' Aunty Bisi glanced at Hassan with a disappointed look. 'Really Hassan? Instead of calming an eight-year-old, you scare her even more by telling her horror stories?'

Hassan's face became an angry scowl and he stomped back into the bedroom.

Aunty Bisi sighed and turned to Anna. She squatted in front of her so she could look her straight in the eyes. 'That's just an old myth, Anna,' she said.

'Here . . .' She tugged her phone out of the back of her shorts and typed something into it.

'Look.' She turned the screen to Anna. Jomi crowded around them with the others and saw an image of a bushbaby that looked just like Ghost. Cute large eyes, pointed ears and a bushy tail.

Aunty Bisi began to read out loud.

'Bushbabies, also called galagos or night monkeys in some regions, are small nocturnal primates native to continental, sub-Saharan Africa. They have enormous, saucer-like eyes, which help them see in low light, and very sensitive bat-like ears with which they can track insects in the dark. They fold their ears back to protect them while jumping through treetops and also in the daytime while resting to keep out sounds that could wake them. They spend most of their lives in trees.

'Bushbabies are impressive jumpers, using their powerful legs and long tails to spring great distances. This allows them to move quickly through the forest to snatch flying insects out of the air.'

'That's cool,' Anna whispered.

Aunty Bisi winked and continued.

'Bushbabies eat fruit, tree gum, insects and small animals like frogs.

'Family groups of two to seven bushbabies often spend the day nestled together in their hollow, but will split up at night to look for food.'

'Do you think Ghost misses her family back home?' Anna asked.

Jomi had been thinking exactly the same thing.

Aunty Bisi glanced at Jomi. 'Well, I'm sure she does. I guess everything here will be new to her. She's probably doing a lot of adjusting at the moment.'

She continued. 'Their natural enemies are snakes, larger owls and wild cats. But the biggest threat for bushbabies are not these predators. The biggest threat for them is their loss of habitat.'

'Oh.' Tanks's voice was a tiny whisper. The air in the little room tensed. In the darkness of their living room, kids avoided each other's eyes and Jomi knew why.

If there was one thing that every single one of them understood, it was loss of habitat. Loss of home. Loss of family.

Aunty Bisi scrolled through her phone, her face seeming even more tired as it was lit by the screen. Her eyes darted from left to right, searching for something. 'Ah, there it is,' she said.

'Bushbabies have a very distinct call which sounds like a crying newborn baby, and is the reason for their name. This distinct cry has led to a lot of myths around the animal, some used to scare children to stay indoors at night.

'So, there we have it!' Aunty Bisi said, tucking away her phone. 'They're just stories used to scare children to stay indoors. In the olden days, people who lived close to forests used to tell their children these stories to make them stay indoors at night. The forests are dangerous places in the dark.'

Aunty Bisi pulled Anna into a hug. 'Have you understood that, Anna? As you can see, there is no need to be worried. There's absolutely nothing supernatural about bushbabies. They are not dangerous and they are animals like any other.'

Anna bobbed her head and grinned. 'And they are also the cutest of all animals. Even cuter than cats.' She wiped her wet cheeks. 'And Jomi is soon going to let me carry her.'

Aunty Bisi patted her back. She got up with a sigh and stared out of the window into the night.

'Jomi, this really cannot happen again. On no account can we risk getting thrown out of this place.'

Jomi gulped. 'I . . . I think maybe she was just lonely or uhm . . . maybe she just wasn't feeling too fine yesterday. I don't know.'

'Well, from what Landlord said it wasn't one or two lonely cries but more like desperate wailing and screeching half the night.'

Jomi stared at the floor. What was wrong with Ghost? She'd really sounded pitiful. Maybe she was missing her forest and her family. Maybe she didn't want the mango tree any more.

'Jomi, I'm sorry, but if this happens again, we'll have to get rid of her.'

He stared at her, his mouth open but no sound coming.

'No!' Tanks cried. 'Aunty Bisi, that's not fair. Ghost is homeless just like us. Her forest was taken down by bulldozers just like mine. We can't just get rid of her!' Tanks was speaking so fast her voice came out in contorted angry gusts.

Aunty Bisi tried to say something but Tanks wouldn't let her.

'Ghost deserves to be taken care of, just like us!'

Aunty Bisi looked even more tired, if that was even possible. She rubbed her forehead, started saying something, stopped. Then started again. 'I could call the zoo to ask . . .'

Jomi shook his head wildly. 'She's a wild animal, she's used to being free. We can't put her into captivity.'

'Yes, but a mango tree is not a home for a bush-baby either. It's very far from being a forest.'

Jomi's eyes filled with tears. She was right. This was never going to work.

'OK, let's see how the next days go. Maybe you're right and she was just feeling ill. Did you look at her this evening to make sure she isn't hurt or something?'

'Yes, but I couldn't find anything wrong.'

Aunty Bisi sighed.

'Children, I really have to get some sleep. I have an early shift tomorrow.'

'Hassan, why was your phone off?' She peered into the bedroom. 'You are meant to be reachable for situations like this!'

'There was no electricity all day, so I couldn't charge it.'

Aunty Bisi sighed again. Today, she sounded like a sighing machine.

'OK, I'll come by tomorrow afternoon right after my shift and you can tell me how the night was.'

Jomi's belly was a twisted coil of copper wire. He could hardly breathe. There was no way he was going to let Aunty Bisi get rid of Ghost. He'd rather pack his things and leave.

He glanced out of the window and into the darkness of the backyard. Two round dots glistened in the darkness, not far from the window. Ghost was staring right at them.

## CHAPTER 28

# NIGHT SHADOWS AND PREDATORS

Jomi tossed and turned. Not a single position was making him sleepy and he had tried out all of them. The only one he hadn't tried yet was sleeping on his head, with his legs up in the air.

He imagined all their hot breaths rising up to the ceiling and condensing up there. Soon it would rain down drops of hot liquid breath. He turned again.

'I can't sleep either,' Tanks whispered.

'I'm worried she will cry again,' he replied.

'Of course she will cry again.' Hassan's voice cut sharply through the quiet room. 'Dogs bark, cats miaow and bushbabies wail like crying babies. It's their nature. They are annoying crybabies that are meant to be in a forest where no one can hear their sniffling and wailing.'

Jomi gripped his little wrapper that lay sweaty and abandoned beside him. He wished Hassan weren't quite so right. But he'd seen something in Ghost's eyes. He'd felt the worry in her trembling limbs. She'd been nervous about something. It wasn't just a cry like a dog barking. He was sure of it. And that's what made his insides twist with worry. That and what Aunty Bisi had said about getting rid of her.

He felt like screaming. The mattress he shared with Prosper was damp and sticky but he buried his face into it and tried to calm down.

She'd been all right earlier in the evening. They'd played with her in the backyard. That had been fun. She'd been her normal self, leaping around in the tree for a bit and then coming down every now and then to perch on Jomi's shoulder. She'd allowed the others to pet her and sometimes she'd stayed briefly on someone else's arm, but the only person she really ever felt comfortable with was Jomi. They'd fed her the spiders they'd caught for her.

Maybe last night had just been a one-time thing. He hoped it with all his heart.

Slowly Jomi finally worried himself to sleep.

Until he jolted back out of it.

He'd dreamt she was screaming again. Only that he hadn't dreamt it. There it was again. A lonely, petrifying wail.

Heads bobbed up around him in the darkness.

'Oh no!' Tanks mumbled.

Anna sniffled. 'I don't want Aunty Bisi to get rid of Ghost. I don't mind if we all go mad. I just want Ghost to stay.'

'Shh, don't worry,' Taiwo whispered, cuddling her.

Jomi grabbed his torch which he'd kept ready beside him. He scrambled up and headed out, Prosper close on his heels.

'Just try and sleep,' Jomi heard Tanks whisper to the others. 'We'll try to calm her down.'

As soon as he entered the living room, he saw her two huge eyes peering in through the slit in the curtains. Two bright saucer eyes, golden-brown and terrified.

He rushed out of the door and Ghost jumped

on to his shoulder. The air outside was as heavy and thick as inside. Why was Ghost's fur so wet?

It hadn't rained.

Had she wet herself while drinking? He walked up to the bowl of water he had placed underneath the benches for her. It was upturned. The water had seeped out and into the earth but the earth around the bowl was dry, as if this had happened hours ago.

Tanks squatted beside him and stroked Ghost's fur. 'Why is she wet?'

'That's exactly what I'm trying to find out here.'

'Her water is gone,' Chuks said, patting the earth like Jomi had done.

Ghost tensed and gave another heart-rending cry. Jomi felt his blood freeze at the sound. Her entire body vibrated with the tremor of it. Goosebumps crawled across his skin and he shivered even though it was hot enough to air-fry an egg.

'Shh,' Tanks whispered and stroked Ghost's back.

'Uff,' Prosper said, wiping his eye with the sleeve of his T-shirt. 'That's the saddest thing I ever heard. My eyes just started leaking all by themselves.'

Ghost cried out again.

'What's wrong, little Ghost?' Chuks whispered.

'Oh Lord!' someone yelled from one of the neighbouring houses.

Jomi stiffened.

'Someone give that possessed child what it wants so we can all rest!' another person called. A window was banged closed with full force.

'What should we do?' Tanks asked. Her eyes darted around in panic. Jomi felt just as terrified as she looked.

'I don't know,' he whispered. He looked around and up into the grey sky. There wasn't even a moon tonight. The sky was too hazy and heavy with humid heat. But the sky was lightening up. It was shortly before morning.

'Talk to us, Ghost,' he whispered. 'Please.' He stared into her eyes, huge and bulging. Ghost lifted her head. She peered up into the tree and back at the house. Had she been trying to get in? It had almost looked like she'd wanted to escape into the house, away from the tree.

Jomi stared at her. It was almost dawn. She was meant to sleep soon. Just like yesterday, her cries had been shortly before dawn.

'We have to check the tree! Yesterday I didn't check her nest. Maybe there's something wrong up there.'

Jomi helped push Tanks up first. Then Prosper.

Ghost still didn't look like she wanted to leave his shoulder or go back up into the tree.

'Can you take care of her?' he asked Chuks who nodded and carefully took Ghost from him. Then he pushed the torch between his teeth and swung himself up with the rope. Tanks and Prosper were already waiting and pulled him up.

Jomi shone his torch around inside the tree. The full, leafy crown was dark and eerie.

'What did Aunty Bisi say yesterday about a bushbaby's natural enemies?' Prosper asked in a wobbly voice.

'Snakes, large owls and wild cats,' Tanks whispered.

'Well, we can remove wild cats from the predator list,' Jomi said. 'Do you think there might be a snake up here?' He wouldn't be afraid to shoo away an owl even if it was a big one. But he wasn't very much a fan of snakes.

'Landlord killed a snake in the yard behind his cartons once. It was a black viper,' Tanks said. 'He said it wasn't a dangerous one but Aunty Bisi forced us to wear shoes for weeks afterwards.'

'Snakes like trees, right,' Prosper said.

'Just make sure you watch where you put your hands and feet,' Jomi said, shining his torch in front of them.

'Maybe we should do this in the daytime,' Tanks said.

Jomi looked around, beginning to feel worried too. He swallowed. 'But we can't expect Ghost to come back up here if there's a predator.'

'OK,' Tanks whispered.

'But we don't even have a machete or something. What do we do if we find a snake?'

Jomi groped around in his pocket until he found his pocket knife. He handed it to Prosper. 'It's not much but better than nothing.'

Tanks broke off two twigs and handed him one. Jomi tucked his into the back of his shorts.

'I just want to check her nest at least.' He

grabbed a branch further up and pulled himself forward. Then he shone the torch around quickly and held his breath. Nothing unusual.

Slowly and warily, they made their way up to the nest they'd built for Ghost. Everything looked fine. Jomi tested the ropes that held the calabash. They were sturdy and tight.

But a strange sound came from the inside of the calabash when he touched it. A gurgling sound.

He shone his torch into the gourd. 'What is this?' he mumbled. Something glistened inside, like water! He reached into it and withdrew his hand immediately, surprised at the cold wetness.

'It's full of water!' he cried, frowning.

'But how is that even possible?' Prosper reached in as well.

'It didn't even rain,' Tanks said. 'And that's why we made sure to lie it down sideways, so it doesn't fill up with rain!'

Suddenly a movement ever so slight caught Jomi's eye. A dark shadow in the gloomier, leafier part of the tree. He shone his torch into the darkness and his breath caught. There, between the leaves, was Ghost's natural enemy.

# CHAPTER 29

# A DIFFICULT STRAY KITTEN

'Hassan!'

'What are *you* doing up here?'

Hassan didn't reply. He just stared at them, his eyes cold and angry. Then he began to scramble down. He thrashed through the branches as he slithered down, fast and not saying a word.

At the bottom of the tree they heard Chuks mumble something in surprise and then the door banged as Hassan entered the house.

For a brief moment Jomi could not move or speak. He was too stunned even to breathe.

Tanks caught herself first. 'That sly, mean devil!' she hissed. 'I'm going to finish him.'

Jomi began to fumble with the knots that held the nest. Tanks held up the torch and Prosper joined him in undoing the ropes.

'Careful Chuks, move aside,' Jomi called down. Then he emptied the water from the gourd with jerky, angry movements.

'He did *what*?'

Aunty Bisi looked like she would burst out of her dress. She paced the living room and since it was so small, it looked like she was walking in tiny circles. Jomi had never seen her angry before. She looked fierce and even though she was a small person, hardly taller than Ivie or Hassan, who were the tallest among them, he felt very happy that she wasn't angry with him.

Suddenly she stopped pacing and faced Jomi. 'How is Ghost now? Did he hurt her?'

'I don't think so, at least I couldn't see anything physically wrong with her,' Jomi replied. 'As soon as Hassan left and we fixed her nest, she hopped into it and slept.'

'Where is Hassan now?'

They shrugged.

She snatched up her phone from the table and poked it sharply to call up the number.

'Hassan?'

Hassan's voice mumbled something on the other end.

'What are you talking about?'

Another round of words on the other end.

Aunty Bisi was shaking her head all the while as if she was hearing something she didn't want to hear.

'I want you to come home, right now, Hassan!'

'No!' This time the reply was short. And loud and clear.

Jomi held his breath. The others stared at Aunty Bisi with eyes that knew exactly what this meant for Hassan.

Aunty Bisi also knew what this meant. She took a deep breath and this time her voice was slower and more careful. Like she was trying to coax a difficult stray kitten into letting her look at its wound. 'Hassan, we can talk things over. I know for some reason you've been having it tough recently. I just wish you would talk to me.'

'No,' Hassan cried again. His voice was a harsh echo in the living room. 'I'm not coming back!'

'Hassan! Hassan!' Aunty Bisi cried, gripping the phone tightly. But he'd cut the connection.

Aunty Bisi turned to face them. They were all standing in an almost straight line in front of her, like silent statues at a road junction. But her gaze was blurred as if she was staring through them and into a faraway distance.

The difficult stray kitten was gone.

# CHAPTER 30

# RAIN AND FLOODS

Jomi sprang up and out of bed. Since he'd discovered Hassan up in the tree, he was always awake at dawn. It was as if his body had switched on an inner alarm clock. Every morning, he climbed up into the tree to check on Ghost. She was always waiting. It was an unspoken agreement between them now that she would not hop off into her nest to sleep until she had told him goodnight for the day. If everything was fine he'd watch her jump safely into the gourd, big saucer eyes, bushy tail and all. Then he'd read and reread his mum's letters and think about her, until the sun was fully out and blazing through the leaves.

This morning when he woke up, something was different. The curtain in their bedroom was raging like the cape of an angry superhero and the air blowing in through the open slit was cold and wet. Rain drummed the window with a thousand fingers.

That was why he'd slept so deeply. For the first time since he'd arrived in Lagos he hadn't tossed and turned half the night, itching with sweat and mosquito bites. It had been a deep, peaceful sleep. He'd even dreamt of his mum for the first time in a long time. He hadn't actually seen her in his dream, but he'd heard her voice. Her warm, re-assuring voice, calling his name.

Jomi dodged his way through the arms and legs scattered around the room and skidded to a halt at the window. The floor beneath the thrashing curtains was completely wet.

The dawning day outside was dark and raging. The scent drifting in from the road was not the usual smell of early traffic, heat and smoke but the pure, heavy scent of earth freshly softened by rain. He pressed his nose into the broken netting and gulped down deep breaths of it. His face was wet in a few seconds. He shut the window as quietly as possible, which wasn't easy because some of the wood splintered every time they closed it.

Jomi stared out for a few more seconds, hypnotized by the sight. The rainy season in Lagos obviously came just like it did back in his village. No quiet announcement in advance, no early premonitions or signs in the air. Suddenly the rain was there like a roaring lion shaking its mane in the wind, howling to make sure everyone knew it had arrived.

Jomi began to shiver. He snatched up his little wrapper from his mattress, covered his shoulders and groped his way out.

It had been a week now since Hassan had left but he could only relax when he'd checked on Ghost. No one had seen Hassan since. Aunty Bisi had tried reaching him but he'd blocked her call. She'd made them look for him in all his usual hang-outs under the big bridge, at the market and near the traffic lights junction where they'd sold mangoes. But they hadn't found him.

Then a couple of days ago they'd even ventured into the agbero quarters at night, although they hadn't told Aunty Bisi about that. Jomi had choked at the bitter smell of cigarettes billowing out of the windows. They'd rubbed their burning eyes as they'd peered into the dimly lit bar. There, through the smoke they'd glimpsed him in a corner, thin and haggard with spiky dreads standing upright on his head. He'd been watching a game of cards, hollering along with the other onlookers. But they'd been too scared to go in or call him.

Jomi felt guilty about Hassan leaving. Aunty Bisi was heartbroken. She'd also searched for him and looked sadder every day. And even though Tanks kept saying how she would box his ears when she got hold of him, Jomi could sense that she was just as worried as the others. He was part of their little bunch and they missed him. Jomi didn't really care about Hassan but he did worry about where he slept. When he thought of his first day alone in Lagos and how he'd sat alone in the abandoned stall for the night, he felt awful for Hassan.

The backyard was still almost completely dark. The tree didn't allow much of the dim light of dawn through. Ghost was on his shoulder in a second. She'd been waiting for him at the threshold of the door and was soaked to the bone. But she didn't seem worried. She was springy and squeaky, hopping around in excitement.

'Rainy season is an exciting time, isn't it,' he said quietly.

His favourite thing in rainy season had been catching esunsun with Tinuke. As soon as the rains came, bringing the winged termites with them, they would set full buckets of water underneath long fluorescent lights to catch the falling esunsun. Aunty Patience would let them fry the delicious winged termites in her pan and they'd eat them in soaked garri.

His belly did a little twist at the memory.

'I'm sure you're also thinking of esunsun. Or do you prefer digging out big fat worms from under palm tree roots? Or juicy snails crawling out of softened earth holes?'

He remembered the smells of the forest after the rain. A deeply rich smell of wood and earth and leaves and nature that could not be described in words. He took a deep breath. The morning air here didn't come close but it was fresher today.

'I'm not sure the rainy season will be the same for you in Lagos, Ghost,' he said, feeling sad for her. 'But we'll make the best of it for now, OK?'

He took a step down and that was when he noticed the ground. Something was very weird about it. It was wobbly. He focused his eyes. Two squarish things that looked like cartons bobbed by. Was he still dreaming?

'Oya-oya, who is that, get down here and help me, boy!'

Jomi stiffened. The harsh voice came from the side of the house.

Ghost was off his shoulder and up in the tree in a second.

A tall man with a slightly bent-over back was wading through a river of water towards him. He hadn't been dreaming. The backyard was flooded. And this was Landlord coming through the flood. He'd seen him once when Aunty Bisi had sent them to get a new pack of candles from him.

'Where are the others, call them, quick-quick!'

'Come quickly, Landlord needs help,' Jomi yelled into the house. Sleepy-eyed faces began to hurry out.

'Oya, carry these boxes to my store,' Landlord called.

He heaved up the dripping boxes that had been stacked into the corner. One at a time he dropped a box on to their heads. Jomi yelped and tried to balance the carton with his hands. Then slowly and with much swaying and stumbling, he managed to wade through the knee-high water towards the front of the house. The others were like zombies, still half asleep. Only Landlord muttered every few seconds in a desperate voice: 'My things! My things!'

By the time the stack was half its original height, Landlord's shop was full.

'Inside there,' he yelled, pointing to their own living room.

They stuffed the remaining cartons into their house until it was also soggy and brimming and they had to walk sideways to get through.

When they'd finished everyone was shivering and cold.

'Take this,' Landlord said, pulling out something from one of the shelves in his store. He dropped two big bags of kuli-kuli and a tin of cocoa into Keni's wet, trembling hands. Landlord was also wet and trembling.

'Where will we sit?' Anna asked as they walked back round the house to their backyard, her voice sounding wobbly. She'd asked exactly what Jomi was thinking.

'Where will we eat?' Taiwo asked. They had stacked the wet cartons all over their table.

'Aunty Bisi will help us sort that out later,' Tanks said.

'Hey, at least we can have a hot drink to warm ourselves up,' Keni said, swinging the tin of cocoa. Anna nodded, her face lighting up just a little.

The backyard looked strangely empty without the stack of boxes in the corner.

Only the wooden pallets on which the boxes had stood remained and they had begun to bob around in the water.

'Boats!' Prosper yelled suddenly, his eyes wide and bulging.

'Boats!' Chuks screamed and dived on one of them. He sank under the water briefly and then bobbed back up, spluttering.

Jomi grabbed another one, threw himself on it and began paddling his hands through the brown, swirling water. The pallet was like a raft and glided forward through the swirl. He squealed as Anna joined him on his boat and they paddled wildly around the yard, giggling every time one of them fell off. No one was cold any more. Paddling and jumping around and giggling had warmed every one up.

Tanks sailed past them, standing upright on her raft and paddling herself forward with a yam pestle.

Jomi stood up slowly as well. Anna squealed as the raft wobbled.

'Aye captain,' Tanks saluted.

Jomi saluted back. They were sailors. Sailors braving whatever storms came their way.

# CHAPTER 31

# THE DIFFERENT USES OF A STURDY CHECKED SHOPPING BAG

'How long will the floods remain?' Jomi asked as they prepared to run out for bole and fresh boiled groundnuts.

Aunty Bisi had come directly from work after Landlord called her to report the carton situation. She had taken a brief look at the mess, handed them the money for dinner and marched over to the store to have a talk with him.

'It's rainy season,' Tanks said. 'As long as it rains almost every day, the water will remain.' She had tied three plastic bags together and was now winding them around her head.

Jomi picked up one of the old colourful checked shopping bags from the corner of the kitchen.

'I already have a bag. These ones are all torn. They're no good any more.'

'Nothing is ever useless,' Jomi said, winking. 'Have you forgotten our dance story?'

She grinned.

'These bags could be perfect raincoats.'

'Huh?'

He found a red-and-white one with a hole at the bottom. 'Ha!' He tugged the spacious square bag upside down and over his head. His head poked out of the hole and he pulled until the bag covered his shoulders.

Tanks grinned at him. 'You look kind of cool. Like one of those space people.'

'Yeah, a checked-shopping-astronaut.'

'Haha, let's go shopping on the moon,' Tanks giggled. She'd entirely covered her head in a huge turban of plastic bags, all the way down to her eyebrows.

Jomi tried not to grin. 'What about the rest of you?' he said.

'Hair is most important. It can't just get wet, like that,' she said. 'You have to take care of it if you don't want it all frizzy and difficult to comb.'

She pointed to his head. 'Your head is sticking out of the bag like a dry coconut. It could also do with some love and care.'

'No, thank you,' Jomi said. He picked up another shopping bag. This one was a blue-and-white checked one that had no handles any more. He searched his pockets for his cutter knife and slit open the bottom.

'Your own astronaut-shopping-raincoat specially made for you. With an extra-big hole for your big head.'

She pushed her turbaned head through and grinned.

At the door, they took a last deep breath before bracing themselves for the journey.

In Lagos the rain didn't sink into the earth like it did back in his village. Here it hovered in deep puddles on the streets and in tsunami splashes that hit you when cars came around corners and in bubbling thick green porridge in street gutters alongside the roads. After only a night and a day of rainfall, every street they walked on was underwater. They ran past cars honking desperately in traffic jams that were worse than usual, cars drowning in mud and potholes the drivers couldn't see. Hawkers who might have still bothered to hold up the hems of their trousers and wrappers in the morning had now given up, allowing their clothes to billow around them as they dragged themselves through the floods.

'Now would actually be a good time to sell something in traffic,' Jomi said through gritted teeth as they crossed the road. The rain was pelting down in torrents, and he was worried that if he opened his mouth while speaking, he would choke.

The cars weren't moving at all. Selling something here now would be perfect. He sighed. If they had something useful to sell.

'Tanks, our dance is coming on nicely but we still don't have any costumes and we still don't have any money for the bus fare. How is this ever going to work?' To his surprise his voice broke and his eyes were burning with hot tears.

Tanks placed a dripping wet hand on his astronaut-raincoat and it made a crackling sound. She looked him right in the eye.

When Tanks did that – looked you right in the

eye – then it made you feel like what she was about to say was the whole truth and nothing but the truth. And that you had to believe it.

'Listen, Jomi, it's going to work. I have a very good belly-feel about it,' she said.

Jomi nodded, believing her.

'I had an idea last night,' she said, also gritting her teeth and speaking through them as the rain hit her face.

'Remember how Anna said that baby in Landlord's shop wanted to have her doll? And the baby's mum wanted to buy it?'

Jomi nodded.

'What if we make more dolls and try to sell them?'

'Oh, do you think we could?'

Tanks nodded. 'We just need Ivie to show us. She won't have time to do them for us, since she works. It took her for ever to finish the doll for Anna. But we could try ourselves if she could show us how, maybe help us do the difficult cutting bits. I can already sew a little.'

'Me too,' Jomi said, slapping his pockets. 'I sewed these on myself.'

He was beginning to feel something tiny and hopeful bubbling in his belly.

'You see.' Tanks shrugged and spread out her hands, like the problem was already solved.

'Thanks, Tanks,' he said. It sounded like he'd said her name twice.

She eyed him, not sure if he was making fun of her.

'I really mean it,' he said. 'I'm glad you're on my team.'

'You mean dance crew,' she said, giving him a fist bump.

They'd already reached Madam B. The roasted plantains were steaming hot over a spluttering grill. Madam Bole's son was fighting to hold up a huge umbrella against the wind and rain.

They paid for a bag of boiled groundnuts and eight bole. One for each of them. Madam B wrapped the hot bole in newspaper and Jomi tucked them under his spacious outfit. A delicious warmth filled the inside of the bag-raincoat.

Tanks grabbed the nuts and they hurried back.

'How did you get your name? I mean without the h and all.'

'My parents can't read or write. At least not very well. So that's what my dad wrote down at the local government place where you get the birth certificate.'

'Oh,' Jomi said.

'But I don't mind, you know. It's number one on my list of special things that happened to me. It's my own very special name so I'm going to be proud of it and I'm going to own it, come what may.' Tanks's voice was firm, almost harsh, like she was daring him or anyone on the planet to say otherwise.

Jomi wished he could also feel so confident about the things he felt and thought and did.

'Better proudly own whatever it is that isn't quite perfect about you than let anyone make fun of you, right?'

Jomi grinned.

'I mean just look at us owning our outfits right now. You're actually walking down this road wearing an astronaut costume. And look at my head, it's probably like a giant yam.'

Jomi burst out laughing. He laughed so hard, he almost let the bole drop.

Tanks bobbed her big head this way and that like she was a yam-headed astronaut in space and they laughed till they were crying.

'But I'm taking my reading lessons with Aunty Bisi very seriously,' Tanks cried as they began to splash forward again. 'One day when I have kids I want to give them a name that is spelt correctly, you know? Or at least spelt the way I actually want it spelt.'

A cold gust of wind swept by, bringing even more rain down. They began to run. As fast as knee-high puddles would allow.

Jomi's pockets clanked and their bag-raincoats crackled with every step. He thought about what Tanks had said. About owning what wasn't so perfect about oneself.

'Do you know what, Tanks,' he cried, rain rushing into his mouth. 'I think I just had an idea for costumes.'

Tanks raised an eyebrow and then her face formed a wide smile. It was a big sly grin, like she knew exactly what he was thinking.

## CHAPTER 32

# CONFESSION

'Goodness, these dolls are really keeping you all busy and quiet today!'

Aunty Bisi dropped a huge pot of steaming sweet-potato pottage on the table. She'd cooked dinner, something which happened rarely since she usually never had that much time. But since Hassan left and with their living room bursting with damp cartons that touched the ceiling, Aunty Bisi was like an agitated mother hen flapping about and worrying over her chicks. She yawned as she set the table.

'Children, could you please leave those dolls now and come have dinner. Wonders shall never end! I never thought I would live to see the day I would need to call you twice for dinner.'

Jomi carefully dropped his needle and the

pieces of cloth he was stitching together. Ivie had cut out the shapes and taught everyone the best stitch to use, which she'd called backstitch. She'd had to write the word down because she hadn't known the sign for it.

Everyone had been so excited about the idea of making dolls and selling them and earning loads of money that they'd all joined in.

'I really am impressed at how creative and motivated you all are. Well done,' Aunty Bisi said.

'Mine is going to be a boy-doll with one very muscly arm,' Prosper said.

'I'm not going to sell mine,' Anna said, clenching hers tightly with one hand and her fork in the other.

'Well, of course you don't need to sell yours,' Aunty Bisi said. 'I told that lady, didn't I?'

'But Tanks said they need all the money they can get!'

'Yeah, but I didn't mean yours, Anna, don't worry,' Tanks interrupted quickly, glancing at Aunty Bisi. 'Aunty Bisi, you didn't forget your laptop right? It's Thursday, so it's *LLD* finals day today.' She was trying to change the topic.

But Aunty Bisi was already on to them. 'You are planning to sell the dolls?'

'Yes, because nobody wants to buy mangoes in traffic and Destiny's Crew need money for the bus fare to Victoria Island,' Anna said.

'*What*?' Aunty Bisi asked.

'Can you just shut your busy mouth for once, Anna!' Tanks hissed.

'Mind your own business, Anna,' Chuks said at the same time.

Anna's bottom lip began to wobble. Everyone went quiet.

'Who is going to VI? Who are Destiny's Crew? And who has been selling mangoes in traffic?'

Jomi dropped his fork and stopped chewing. OK, they were in big trouble. He glanced at Tanks. She was biting her lip and avoiding Aunty Bisi's intense gaze.

'What is going on here? I want an answer right now!'

'*We* are Destiny's Crew,' Prosper said, crossing his arms across his chest as he said it.

'We have a cool choreo and we are going to audition for *LLD*,' Chuks said.

'We are helping Jomi find his mum,' Tanks blurted.

Aunty Bisi shook her head and rolled her eyes. 'That sounds like a nice thing to want to do.' She glanced at Jomi. 'I mean . . .' she frowned. 'How does auditioning even help Jomi find his mum? You are all not making any sense at all.'

'My mum watches every single *LLD* show. She told me in her letter,' Jomi said.

Aunty Bisi nodded slowly. 'I see.'

But then she shook her head again. 'I'm sure you all realize this is not going to work. I'm sorry to have to be the one to spoil your plans. But as the adult here I have to protect you from disappointment and from danger as well.'

'But we can—'

'But Aunty Bisi—'

Everyone started talking at once.

Aunty Bisi raised her hands and shook her head firmly. 'Children, this is not a joke or a game. You can't just think you can pop by the biggest TV show in Lagos and dance and win.'

'But Nneka Oji said anyone and everyone can take part!' Prosper said. His voice was high-pitched and panicked.

Jomi felt like he was falling. Slowly but steadily. He had that weird sensation in his belly like when you're jumping down from a high tree, and the voices seemed to be fading away like if he was falling further and further away from them. Further away from his dream. He had to fight. He had to convince Aunty Bisi. But he felt weak.

'We don't have to win, we only want to get in,' Chuks was saying. His eyes were wide and fearful, his forehead furrowed.

'We already promised Jomi we would help him,' Tanks said. 'We have to keep our promise.'

'Yes, but you need a decent dance, you need proper costumes! We don't have that! I don't have any money for costumes for you! Did you see those glittery leather costumes your Danstars were wearing last week? Those kids look like they go to a private dance school and they probably practised their dance every day for weeks.'

'We've been practising every day for weeks and we already have costumes,' Tanks snapped.

But Aunty Bisi was shaking her head very, very firmly.

'Nobody is going on a bus all the way to VI for any auditions! And definitely, nobody is selling anything in traffic. I've told you before that it's dangerous. And that's final.'

Aunty Bisi peered at everyone to make it clear how seriously she meant it.

But she didn't look at Jomi.

'Eat up, kids,' she said, instead. 'Your *LLD* show is starting in a few minutes. I thought you didn't want to miss the finals.'

She got up abruptly. 'I'll set up the laptop.'

She squeezed through the cartons to get her bag. Then with the laptop in her hand she suddenly stood very still. She was staring at the room, the cartons everywhere, like she was seeing them for the first time. She swallowed. Jomi saw her throat wobble. And then . . .

Aunty Bisi actually kicked one of the cartons.

'We can't even move in this place!'

She was breathing heavily.

'You know what, children, we are not going to squeeze around in here like boxed-up sardines to watch *LLD*. The situation here is unacceptable. I pay rent here and I don't care if it's only short-term, this is not acceptable!'

Jomi had never seen her like this.

Aunty Bisi whipped around and snatched her big bunch of keys off the table.

'Children, get up, oya-oya, follow me.'

They walked out into the backyard in a quiet line through the little gate round to the front. No one spoke, not even Anna. She just clutched her doll to her chest and held on to Ivie.

Aunty Bisi marched straight to Landlord's shop. It was locked and dark since it was late. It looked almost ghostly. The lock snapped loudly as she turned the key.

'We're watching it here today,' Aunty Bisi hissed.

Jomi didn't feel like watching *LLD* any more. Not if he couldn't audition there to find his mum. He felt faint. His belly ached.

They crowded in and huddled together on the floor in front of the shelf with the exercise books and pencils.

'Careful, children, don't touch or break anything OK?' Aunty Bisi whispered.

Then she switched on Landlord's shop TV and

the shop lit up. The *LLD* music was playing already.

Someone took his hand and pressed it gently. It was Tanks.

Jomi's eyes filled with tears.

## CHAPTER 33

# A BOLD MOVE

The Danstars were out. They had lost. It was over for them. Gasps fizzed through the darkness around Jomi.

'Oh no!' Prosper whispered.

The Danstars cried bitterly and Nneka Oji hugged them while they cried, not caring that their tears wet her dazzling purple-and-silver dress.

The Danstars' thirteen-year-old crew leader, Seyi, wiped his face and took the microphone. 'I'm so proud we did this,' he said. 'No one believed in us as much as we did. That's the only reason we came this far.'

Suddenly Jomi couldn't stand it any longer. He jumped up. 'Aunty Bisi, you don't believe in us,' he said. He was surprised at how steady his voice

239

came out. On the inside he didn't feel steady at all. He walked over to the shop counter where she sat.

'You don't believe in us, that's why,' he repeated. 'But . . . but we believe in us,' he said.

'Right?' he asked, turning back.

'Yes, we believe in us,' Tanks, Chuks and Prosper said, scrambling up to join him.

Aunty Bisi sighed and muted the television.

'You should at least see our dance before you say no and write us off,' Jomi said.

'It won't change the fact that we just don't have the means to—'

'Please Aunty Bisi, just let us show you at least,' Tanks cut in.

Aunty Bisi looked around and then nodded. 'OK, show me. We'll do it here.' She put the light on.

'Yay!' they yelled excitedly. Jomi's heart was thudding so hard, he could hardly breathe. They'd been practising every day for weeks, but were they ready? Would Aunty Bisi like their dance? What if they were being silly?

But Prosper and Chuks were dragging him out already.

'The music,' Tanks said.

'And our costumes,' Chuks said.

A couple of minutes later, they were back in the store, wearing their upturned checked shopping-bag costumes. They'd all found Jomi's idea for costumes cool.

Aunty Bisi sat rigid with hands in her lap at the counter. Taiwo, Keni, Ivie and Anna stood beside her like a real audience. They had moved the newspaper rack and the gift stand out of the way and created a stage in the middle of the shop.

Destiny's Crew were ready to perform. They went into their starting positions.

Jomi glanced at the others and when everyone nodded, he made a sign to Keni to press start on the cassette player.

Jomi began to edge forward, dancing slow legwork moves. Then he bent over and his costume ripped open at the back as planned. They'd cut open the back of the bag, so he could slip in and out of it easily. 'Thro'way,' he cried and held up the ripped bag, pointing at the tear while moving his body in tune with the music. Then he made a flinging movement and fired his legs along in Awilo style. The others stepped forward, dancing in sync around him and waving their arms in exaggerated shock that he had thrown away his costume.

Their audience began cheering and clapping.

Then they all moved backwards, leaving only Tanks in front. 'Pick up,' she cried and began twisting her waist and hips while picking up Jomi's costume. As she danced her way upright in umlando style, she shook her bum better than even the Danstars.

Their little audience was hollering and clapping to the beat. Jomi stole a quick glance at them. Aunty Bisi looked serious, her face unreadable. Jomi felt a short tug in his belly, but only briefly. He danced on behind Tanks, not caring. He was going to dance his very best and they would give Aunty Bisi and the others the best show they could. He could feel the vibes like never before. His entire body was on fire with the beats and he was one with the music. And he could sense that the others were feeling the same.

Now Tanks danced slowly, working her way backwards towards Chuks. She twirled around and held out the costume to him. From the corner of his eye, Jomi saw Chuks snatch the costume and wave it.

Suddenly Chuks leapt forward like someone being attacked by gbomo-gbomo. Jomi's breath caught as Chuks hurled himself forward, looking like he was about to stumble. But he wasn't stumbling. He was actually doing a front flip. This hadn't been part of the choreo!

Jomi squeezed his eyes shut, waiting for the crash. But there was none. Chuks landed with a thud and standing firmly upright, he yelled 'Fix'am' like his life depended on it. His big square costume crackled as he began to do his shaku-shaku. He worked the ripped costume in his hand like he was fixing it to the rhythm. His movements were rigid and edgy, because that was how Chuks danced. And with him doing the fixing movements, it was perfect. He looked like a dancing cube in his square costume. Their audience was cheering and cheering. Jomi caught Tanks's gaze as they danced their accompanying Fix'am movements behind Chuks. Her eyes were popping in amazement. Chuks who had said he didn't want a solo. He was fantastic.

Chuks danced back in line and passed Jomi's costume to Prosper who now came forward. 'Shine'am,' he cried, rippling his body with supple gwara moves. Then he rubbed his hands over the torn costume, shining it and then over his entire body as well until it was as if even the air around him was shining. Prosper could make his body look like rubber and all the while he was doing Happy Feet and letting his feet glide smoothly to the left and back to the right.

The audience was going wild. Jomi felt a wave of warmth and pride in his belly for all of them. They had practised so well. No one had made any mistakes. There had even been spectacular surprises.

Prosper held out Jomi's 'fixed' and 'shined' costume and the others danced towards him. Together they helped Jomi slip back into it and then circled around him, doing the last choreo in Skelewu. Jomi gave his very best for this last bit and he could feel the same energy in the others. They were all desperate to convince Aunty Bisi.

Right on cue at the last beat, Tanks did her split in front of them while Prosper and Chuks grabbed Jomi's waist and hoisted him up between them. Jomi threw back his head and spread his arms for the dramatic end of their dance.

Ivie, Anna and the twins screamed and whistled and clapped and pounded Landlord's counter as if it were a drum.

The others had never really seen the whole dance, only little bits here and there, while they'd practised.

Destiny's Crew high-fived each other with wide grins. All of them still panting and trying to catch their breath. Jomi glanced at Aunty Bisi. His nervous heart was not making it easy for him to calm down. The others crowded around him, also waiting for Aunty Bisi to say something.

But she didn't.

Instead, to his horror, she put a hand to her mouth and made an awful sound.

She was crying.

Everyone crowded around Aunty Bisi. Jomi's belly was drawn tight and he felt close to tears too. What did it mean? Would she allow them to go to the audition?

'Come here, children,' she said, pulling them all into her small arms one by one. 'I love you all so much. If you only knew how happy I would be to . . . give you everything you need . . . a really good home and schooling . . . and . . .'

'But did you like our dance?' Tanks asked, her voice sounding muffled in Aunty Bisi's armpit.

'It was beautiful. And perfect,' Aunty Bisi cried.

Jomi let out a huge breath.

'I love your message. I love the fight in the message, in the dance. How nothing and no one needs to be thrown away or abandoned – how things can be picked up and fixed and cared for and made to shine again.'

'Really?' Tanks asked, hopping about as she usually did when she was excited.

Aunty Bisi nodded. 'And the costumes are perfect too.' Her eyes filled with tears again.

'I am so proud of you,' she said. 'I can't believe you did that all on your own.'

Tanks glanced at Jomi, her eyes all smiley and her

legs all jumpy. He could hardly keep still himself.

'So, can we go to Victoria Island if we get enough money for the bus fare?' he asked her.

She shook her head. 'I'm sorry, I can't let you go to VI alone on a bus. You could get lost or into trouble all by yourselves.'

Jomi's heart sank into his belly and he sighed. What use was it that she liked their dance if she wouldn't let them go?

'But . . .' Aunty Bisi said. 'I'll think of a way to get you there. You just have to audition!'

'Yayy!' They squealed and hugged each other.

'Wait!' Aunty Bisi said and flipped the sound of the TV back on. 'They're saying it right now.'

The show was over. Nneka Oji was speaking. 'Don't forget that anyone and everyone can audition. In six days, on Friday, our three-day live auditions will begin at our LLD Plaza in Victoria Island. So, if you want to be one of our next contestants then do pop by and show us what you have. Show us your shaku!'

Aunty Bisi switched off the TV.

'OK children, I'll think of something. But like I said, I don't want to hear of anyone selling anything in traffic. If your dolls turn out nice, like Ivie's doll, then I'll ask Landlord if he might agree to sell them in his shop.'

'Oh wow!' Prosper cried.

Aunty Bisi raised a finger. 'They have to be really good, though.'

They tidied the shop, putting everything back the way it was, and Aunty Bisi locked up with a clack.

'Very quietly, children,' she whispered, looking up to the other houses. 'It's late now, we don't want to disturb any neighbours.'

'Wait, Jomi.' Aunty Bisi held him back while the others went round to the yard.

'Jomi, you do know, even if it works, and your dance gets you in – which is not sure – I mean, I love it, really . . .'

She sighed. 'What I mean to say is, there's no guarantee your mum will see it and that she'll come to find you. I . . . I don't want to take your hopes away, I just don't want you to put them too high up, OK?'

Jomi nodded. He couldn't trust his voice right now.

Aunty Bisi laid an arm over his shoulder and squeezed him gently. 'I'm definitely keeping all my fingers and toes crossed for you and I'll pray for you. I really hope it happens.'

Jomi nodded. They had reached the backyard. He glanced up into the tree.

'Where is she today?' Aunty Bisi asked.

He made to whistle but Ghost was already swishing down through the leaves. She dropped on to his shoulder like a bullet and Aunty Bisi laughed quietly.

The light in their living room went on and seeped out into the backyard. Ghost hid in the shadow of Jomi's neck.

Suddenly there was a scream from inside. Then a rush of steps.

Jomi darted in after Aunty Bisi. Ghost sprang off his shoulder and back into the tree, preferring to remain outside in the dark.

And there sitting in the midst of the cartons was a familiar face staring at everyone with angry red eyes.

Hassan.

# CHAPTER 34

# HASSAN

Anna rushed up to Hassan and threw her little arms around him. He patted her stiffly. Jomi and the others stood awkwardly, not sure how to be around him. He looked distraught and his eyes were cold and unfriendly.

'Where were you all?' Hassan hissed. 'I thought you'd left.' His voice broke. 'I thought someone else had moved in.' He pointed to the cartons and his mouth crumbled.

'Everyone, go into the bedroom please,' Aunty Bisi said quietly. 'I would like to speak to Hassan alone.'

Jomi left the room with the others. No one spoke. Only Anna sniffed and whispered quietly. 'Will he stay now? I don't want him to be mad at Jomi any more. I don't want Hassan to go away again!'

They arranged themselves on their mattresses, staring at the door. They might as well have stayed, because even though Aunty Bisi spoke quietly, they could hear every word.

'Hassan, what is going on?'

No reply.

'I can't believe you would disappear for days on end, ignoring my calls.'

'The phone broke.'

Aunty Bisi sighed.

'I am sorry,' Hassan said. 'I messed up.'

'You definitely did. You have been horrible to Jomi and to Ghost since they came.'

Jomi's breath caught at the sound of his name. Why did Hassan hate him so much? He'd been mean to him from the very first day he'd met him.

'And even going to such lengths,' Aunty Bisi continued. 'Climbing trees at night instead of sleeping in bed? How could you be so mean to that animal? And so absolutely irresponsible and reckless? I can't believe you would risk us all getting thrown out!'

'*Us* getting thrown out?' Hassan interrupted sharply. '*We* would get thrown out, not you!'

Silence.

'You never forgave me for moving out.'

Silence.

'You know, I am doing my very best for all of you.' Aunty Bisi's voice broke. 'Don't I also deserve a life? Don't I deserve to be loved, to have a husband?'

Silence.

'You have been acting so strangely these past weeks, Hassan, and I want to know what is wrong. You've always been so mature for your age, so responsible. But I do not recognize you any more. Have you even considered any of the things I suggested last time we talked? Have you tried finding another job? It was a lot of hard work to find a mechanic workshop willing to take in a fourteen-year-old. It was such a fine place and you gave up after a week! You could have told me if you didn't want training as a mechanic and I would have looked for something else.'

Silence.

'Will you just talk to me, Hassan!'

'I don't need any fine-fine workshop like that one,' Hassan snarled. Jomi and the others jumped.

'I want to repair cars, not write down lists of spare parts and assist for inside shine-shine office.'

'But that's part of the job. That's how life is, there are often things you might not like doing, but you do them because that way you get to do other things you really love.'

'Well, I don't need fine workshop like that and I don't care if I don fall your hand and if you are tired of me.'

'What are you talking about, I am not tired of you.'

'All I keep hearing is how I'm old enough, how I'm the oldest, how I should be responsible, how I'm fourteen now. And now that Jomi don join us, we are too many here. You cannot feed us, but no worry, I know I'm the oldest and I have to leave. I'm staying with my friend Dapo now.'

'What in heaven's name are you talking about? Who ever said you would have to go just because you are the oldest?'

'You said we have to find a job, you said we have to start planning our future and start earning money. And I heard you telling your friend for phone that tings are getting tight and you no fit feed us any more. So, I'm going to go. You have your perfect Jomi now who can fit read and be your special teaching assistant. You no need me anyway.'

'Jomi doesn't have anything to do with this. And you were the one who refused to take part in lessons. That's why I thought a job would be best for you. I know my lessons are probably too simple for you but I have so little time and I also have to teach the others the easier stuff. I mean you could have helped me, like Jomi offered to do. You could have taken over teaching the younger ones how to read in my absence, then I would have had more time for you.'

'I *can't read*!' Hassan screamed. 'I'm not a fine-fine boy like Jomi who finish primary school. My father lost him job when I was seven. I never even see inside of classroom. Who suppose pay school fees or buy school books or uniform? My mother get four children and na me be the oldest. So when

254

I reach ten, I join the kids on the streets to find money and to take care of myself.'

Jomi heard a sharp sob.

'So, anyway, you no need to worry, I'm used to being the oldest, I can take care of myself.'

'But . . . but why did you tell me you could read, Hassan?' Aunty Bisi's voice was gentle and sad.

'Because you said reading is the most important thing a person must fit to do. You said reading gives us dignity. And I no want you to think I don't have dignity.'

'Oh, Hassan. Of course, I wouldn't think anything like that of you. I only wanted to make you all understand how important being able to read is. I can't believe you really think I would put you back on the streets?' Aunty Bisi's voice broke again. 'All I want for all of you is that you have some form of training so you can have a good future!

'And I would never send you away. Even if we had twenty kids here, all stacked on top of these stupid cartons here. We would find a way.

'OK?'

Silence.

'Come here, my big boy!' Aunty Bisi said, almost too quiet for them to hear.

Now Jomi heard sniffing and then it was quiet again.

'Jomi!'

He went rigid.

'Jomi!' Aunty Bisi called again. 'Come here please.'

They were sitting beside each other on a carton. Aunty Bisi had an arm around Hassan's shoulders. Hassan's phone was on the carton in front of them. Jomi could see the long crack across the screen even from where he stood.

Aunty Bisi pushed Hassan gently and he stood up. 'I'm sorry, Jomi. I no nice to you and to Ghost. I was worried that I had to go because of you.'

Jomi nodded slowly. 'Ghost didn't deserve that you hurt her,' he said.

'I didn't hurt Ghost, I swear. I even went up the first time to play with her because I find her cute. But she didn't like me. I guess she remembered that I was mean to you the first time we met.

'And so, I filled her nest with water.' He looked

really ashamed. 'I'm sorry . . . I didn't hurt her sha, I promise, I just wanted you both to leave. But I won't go near her again, I swear.'

'OK, I believe you.' Jomi felt relief flood his body as he said the words. Even though he was still angry with Hassan for what he'd done, at least he understood why he had done it. Hassan had been afraid to lose his home. That was something Jomi could definitely relate to. And now, he just wanted an end to all the quarrels and worries.

'I can fix that,' he said to Hassan, pointing at the broken phone. He'd practised replacing screens on tons of old phones from his scrap hill.

'For real?' Hassan asked, with a sheepish smile.

'Yes, I have superglue, so all we need is a replacement screen. And I know where we can get that.'

'Wonderful,' Aunty Bisi cried, clapping her hands together. 'Now that that's cleared up, I just had an idea. Children, where are you?'

Aunty Bisi had not even finished her sentence when all the kids popped their heads out of the bedroom door.

'Yes? Yes, Aunty Bisi? What idea?'

'I have a plan for how to get you to the auditions!'

# CHAPTER 35

# LLD PLAZA, VICTORIA ISLAND

'Third Mainland Bridge has to be the longest bridge in the world,' Chuks said. His voice came out funny because his nose was squashed flat against the window of Mr Folarin's minibus. Jomi was sitting at the window on the other side doing the same thing.

Mr Folarin was Aunty Bisi's husband. He'd agreed to drive them to Victoria Island along with his passengers. She'd warned them to behave themselves at least ten times. Mr Folarin had recently lost his dream job and now had to drive a minibus until he got a new dream job. He didn't like driving a minibus or any bus at all. And he normally never went as far as Victoria Island. But he'd agreed to drop them off and pick them up afterwards because Aunty Bisi never had days off because of all her jobs.

Now Mr Folarin's bus was racing them across the lagoon on a never-ending bridge to Victoria Island, which was so far away it definitely looked like the end of the world. And the end of the world was a magical place of tall buildings that touched the sky. It stood in a mist of blues. Blue waters that sometimes looked turquoise-blue, sometimes deep dangerous marine-blue and sometimes a lazy brownish-blue. And everywhere Jomi looked the waters spread out to touch the blue sky. Even the sky that hovered above Victoria Island looked different. Softer than the harsh one they saw every day. It was a gentle baby-blue, so soft, like a giant pillow.

'Not the longest bridge in the world,' Mr Folarin said. 'It used to be the longest in Africa though. Until the Egyptians built a longer one. As if having the highest pyramids was not enough for them.'

'Well, it's definitely the longest I have ever seen,' Chuks mumbled in a dreamy voice.

'Will you stop talking like a love-struck

dummy,' Tanks hissed. Jomi could feel the stiffness of Tanks's little frame beside his. She was nervous, even though she would never admit it. He held out a fist to her and she bumped it with hers.

'I'm excited,' he said.

She nodded. 'We go smash am!'

She lifted the lid of his rucksack and peered in. 'She's still sleeping,' she said.

'Ghost sleeps like a log in the daytime,' he said. He'd taken her with him. Aunty Bisi had wanted to stop him but he'd told her his mum would come immediately after the auditions and he would go with her. Aunty Bisi hadn't looked very convinced when he'd told her. She'd given him a slip of paper with her telephone number. 'Give this to someone at *LLD*, any staff or security after your performance. Just in case your mum doesn't come . . . I mean ehm if she doesn't come on time, before you have to leave. Then they could give her my number.' She'd looked kind of sad, so he'd hugged her very tight.

'I wish this bridge would end,' Prosper said. He was holding his belly and looking like he'd just eaten beans that had spent the night outside the fridge.

'Hey, boy, you are not going to throw up in my bus are you?' Mr Folarin said sharply. He began to rustle around in the pocket of his door and held up a plastic bag. 'Hold this in case you need it,' he said, passing it behind him. Hassan was sitting next to him, and Mr Folarin's sleeve caught in his hair. He ducked away from Mr Folarin's armpit and bumped into the frilly arm of the big woman beside him. 'Sorry, Ma,' he muttered when she looked down at him with a frown.

Hassan's face in the back mirror had Jomi stifling a laugh in spite of how nervous he was.

He looked like the sausage in a sausage roll, almost completely invisible in the front row. He'd run up to the front of the bus and snatched the front seat for himself as soon as Mr Folarin arrived. He'd looked all smug when the others had sat in the middle row of the bus. But then Mr Folarin had picked up more passengers before driving to Victoria Island. Three had taken their seats in the back row and then the largest passenger of all, a big woman dressed in bright green-and-red ankara with extra-large frilly sleeves, had squeezed herself in front with Hassan.

Prosper took the bag from Mr Folarin. 'Thank you,' he mumbled weakly.

Tanks took one of Prosper's hands and held it firmly.

'I don't remember the last time I was in a car,' Prosper whispered.

'I know,' Tanks said quietly. 'I haven't been in one in a long time either.'

Slowly, the end of the world lost its magical feel and began to look more like a real-life city, with roads and cars and dots of people. They were getting close to their destination. Jomi couldn't believe how huge Lagos was. The first part of their journey on the mainland had gone on for over an hour through traffic and crowds of people. More people than he would have thought possible. Every new busy street or crowded market he'd seen had reminded him of how impossible it would ever be to find his mum here.

He had only this one chance. One shot at finding his mum and making everything turn out right. If this plan didn't work, then that was it. He would never find her.

The closer they got to the end of the bridge, the tighter things began to feel. The traffic thickened again and the sky-scraping buildings grew taller and taller until Jomi couldn't see their tops through the bus windows any more. It felt like they were closing in on him. The blues and the softness of the atlantic and the skies were gone so that all that remained was the grey harshness of asphalt roads and concrete and specks of something a little lighter or darker in between. These were the highest buildings he'd ever seen. It was as if the flooded, potholed, steaming market part of Lagos he had seen up till now was the little loud snot-faced brother of Victoria Island. And now they were getting to meet the stylish and elegant taller sibling who was looking down at them. Jomi gulped. A wave of worry twisted his belly and he glanced at the plastic bag in Prosper's hands. He hoped he wouldn't need it.

They arrived and it immediately felt much too soon. Jomi's heart pounded his ribcage like it wanted to make a hole in it to escape back to the safety of Aunty Bisi's little place with its tiny yard, where the only tall things were friendly mango trees.

The LLD Plaza had been lit by soft, glowing lights on television. But in real life it was still daylight, and the imposing white building with tall windows and stylish curves looked harsh and uninviting. Two long rows of flowery shrubs framed the driveway that led up to wide elegant stairs, which would take contestants through to the grand open doors of the building. The drive-way was filled with crowds of people already. There was a long queue of colourfully dressed groups of people. People of all ages in all sorts of outfits and costumes.

Mr Folarin glanced at the building with doubt-ful eyes and then back at them. 'You kids know what you are doing, sha?' He seemed just as intimidated by the building as Jomi felt.

Tanks nodded for all of them.

'I can't park so you have to get out here.'

Jomi grabbed his rucksack and scrambled out with the others. They stood in a row facing the building, no one ready to take the first step. Cars began sounding their horns behind Mr Folarin's minibus.

'Good luck,' he called before driving off.

'Oh my days!' Hassan said, pushing in behind them and spreading his arms across their shoulders. 'Well, this is amazing.' He let go of them, pulled out his phone and began taking selfies. 'Mehn I go post fantastic pictures for my new followers.' He posed and took some more.

'Jomi, even though you be real pain in the niash, I will be forever grateful to you for fixing my phone,' he said, snapping away.

Jomi smiled in spite of his nervous belly.

'Hassan, this is not what we came for,' Tanks hissed. 'You only have one important job here today, which you better not mess up! The moment Jomi rips off his costume, you have to press play, that's it! And better make sure your friend's loudspeaker is on!'

'So clear that Tanks was going to spoil my show,' Hassan grumbled.

'OK peeps, hurry along now. There are more and more people coming in. We no wan carry last,' Hassan said, suddenly remembering that

Aunty Bisi had said she was relying on him to keep an eye on things.

Tanks rolled her eyes and followed him.

But she popped out her little notepad as she walked and scribbled into it with her tiny pencil.

A day like this was definitely special enough for Tanks's list. 'Tanks, you never told me – what happens when you reach one hundred on your list?' Jomi asked.

'It doesn't really need to get to one hundred. That's just when I'm going to give up.'

'Give up what?'

'Give up hoping that it will happen.' She glanced at him and lowered her voice. 'My biggest wish is to go back to school one day. A real school, not just lessons with Aunty Bisi.' She bit her lip. 'I love Aunty Bisi . . . I don't mean to sound ungrateful . . .'

'I know what you mean,' Jomi said with a sad smile.

'Anyway, so I just thought if lots of really special things can happen to me, then the possibility of that one wish coming true should also be high, right?'

Jomi nodded although he wasn't too sure how this made sense.

'So that's why I keep this list, to remind myself that special things happen and that my wish could come true one day.'

'And you will stop at one hundred?'

She looked away quickly and nodded. 'If I reach one hundred and it hasn't happened, then I'll give up hoping.'

'I don't think we should ever give up hope,' Jomi said.

'Hope is like an elastic band. You can stretch it very far, but one day it will break.' Tanks avoided his gaze as she said this. Then she suddenly clapped her hands. 'But maybe after today I won't need my list any more?' She wiggled her eyebrows, prodded him with her elbow and then skipped forward to join the others.

'Everyone's already wearing their costumes,' Prosper said.

Jomi glanced at the queue that went all the way up the driveway. There was a sort of checkpoint at the bottom of the steps, which led up to the entrance. Purple lights shone inside the grand doors. Jomi couldn't wait to walk through them.

The mood was buzzing. People were giggling and laughing or chanting something. It didn't matter if the dance crews were kids or grown-ups. Everyone was excited. Some people were already dancing and showing off their moves.

But Prosper was right: they were all wearing their costumes already.

'Their costumes are all so fine,' Chuks whispered and glanced at the bundle of red-and-white and blue-and-white checked shopping bags that Prosper clutched tightly.

'Yeah, but none are as creative as ours,' Tanks said. She grabbed one of the bags and pulled it over her head with a determined tug.

'She's right though,' Prosper said. 'They have fine-fine costumes and glittery, uniform colours but nothing creative. Most of them are just normal clothes, only that they're stylish. Maybe we'll get some points for that.'

But Jomi couldn't reply. He didn't feel like he could even make a single sound come out of his throat. He'd never felt so out of place in his entire life. He didn't trust this whole shiny part of

Lagos. He felt like they were flathead screws among a bunch of star screws and soon someone would find out they didn't belong.

He took a deep breath. At least no one was staring at them. Everyone was too excited. The queue was edging forward and they were gradually approaching the entry point now. It was growing dark. The lights on the outside of the building suddenly went on and the letters LLD lit up.

The driveway also lit up brightly and a thrilled wave went through the crowd. Some people clapped. Jomi's heart thudded. They were really here! They were actually going to do this! Only two more groups were in front of them. Then they would reach the registration point where the security check would let them through. It was that easy.

Tanks caught his eye and bumped shoulders with him. Their costumes crackled. 'We're owning it, we'll show them,' she said.

A set of twin ladies behind them, wearing golden jumpsuits, began stretching.

Prosper immediately began flexing his arm

muscles. 'We should also start warming up,' he said.

Hassan was chatting with a girl behind the golden twins. She had lots of make-up on and shiny red lips. Hassan kept brushing his spiky hair back with his hand. 'That's how to make girls like you,' he'd once told them.

Prosper nudged Chuks. They giggled, covering their mouths. 'Ugh,' Chuks said.

'Yeah, this is Destiny's Crew, my dance crew,' Hassan was saying. 'I'm their manager.'

Tanks rolled her eyes and Prosper mimicked him. They burst out laughing.

'Where the hell do you ragamuffins think you are going?'

Three wide, muscly-armed security men stood in their way. They were next in line and the question was directed at them.

Jomi felt his legs weaken.

'We are Destiny's Crew,' Tanks said after a few seconds.

'I don't care if your name is President's Crew. You are not going anywhere.'

'What? But why?' Tanks asked. Her voice was tiny. As tiny as Jomi felt.

'Well, look at you,' the middle one said. He was chewing a huge wad of gum that kept popping out at the side of his mouth.

'What the hell is this?' He pointed at them and the other men laughed.

'These are our costumes. It's part of our theme. Our theme is about—' Tanks continued.

But the chewing-gum man cut her off. 'Spare me the details and just move out of the way, OK!'

'Next!' he called to the group behind them.

'But Miss Nneka Oji said anybody and everybody can take part,' Jomi said, finally finding his voice. He sounded brittle as if his throat was layered with sandpaper.

'Are you anybody?' The chewing-gum man had a nasty sneer.

He turned to his colleagues. 'Look at these nobodies here, saying they want to enter the show. Did Nneka say nobodies can enter too?

'Common will you gerrara here before I kick you out,' he barked.

'But sir, Miss Oji did say the show was free for all to enter!' one of the golden jumpsuit twins called. Her twin also said something but the muscled men shook their heads firmly.

Jomi's breath was refusing to go deep any more. He could only manage short raspy gasps and his chest hurt.

They weren't going to get in.

Everything had been for nothing.

## CHAPTER 36

# THRO'WAY

'I . . . need . . . to . . . find . . . my . . . mum.' Jomi repeated it like a mantra over and over again as Tanks pulled him to the side.

'Oya, out of the way! Allow the next contestants to go in, jareh,' a voice shouted.

The better, richer contestants, Jomi thought. The ones with polished shoes and shiny costumes and uniforms.

'It's not fair,' he whispered.

Tanks's eyes were bright with tears as she tried to pull him on. But he didn't want to leave. He wanted to walk up those stairs like the others and go into those doors to the purple lights. He wanted to go in and dance so his mum would see him and come for him.

They had come this far. They were so close,

they could almost see the stage. Somewhere in there, just through those tall doors, maybe around a corner was the stage with purple lights and the camera. Finding his mum was only a stone's throw and a dance away. And yet he wouldn't be able to. Because he was a nobody.

He'd always known it deep down inside of him. Deeper than his deep pockets could go, he'd known that all that shining and fixing and repairing was for nothing. A broken thing was still a broken thing no matter how much you shined it. That mean old crack would still shine through. Its outline would be there, to remind you. The proof that it was crap. Rubbish. Useless.

Jomi suddenly felt like he was choking. He was suffocating inside the stupid shopping-bag costume. He set down his rucksack and ripped the annoying thing off and over his head.

Hassan, who had been busy toasting the girl with too much make-up and hadn't even noticed what happened, darted over with wide eyes, his phone in his hand.

'Oh, sorry, I didn't realize it's time already . . .' he whispered. A second later their dance song was blasting loud and thunderous from the loudspeaker in his pocket.

Jomi startled.

'No!' Prosper whispered. 'Not here! They've thrown us out, Hassan.'

But the music was playing so loud that Hassan couldn't hear him.

With all the force he could muster up, Jomi flung the annoying costume on to the ground. He'd done this hundreds of times while practising. But for the first time his motion of flinging it into the dirt felt true. It was over. All those years he'd spent gathering things and fixing and shining and polishing them were over. He wasn't deceiving himself any more. They weren't worth it. He wasn't worth it. The chewing-gum man was right. He was a nobody.

'Thro'way!' he cried. And he didn't care that tears were pouring down his face and that people were beginning to stare. He danced the Thro'way dance for everyone to see.

A circle formed around them.

Jomi danced Thro'way for them with all the pain he felt. And with each step, with each move, something cracked inside him.

When he finished, he looked up and jerked back in surprise. People were cheering for him and Tanks was standing right in front of him as if she was ready for a battle. She was staring him down, her chest heaving. She had that determined look on her face. The one she always had on when she thought she knew better. She knew exactly what he was thinking and she wanted to tell him he was wrong.

She made a sudden move right in his face. A quick slide-attack. Then she began to twirl her way down to the ground, each move answering him as she danced to pick up the costume.

The crowd went wild around them. People began hollering and pushing to join the circle.

'Pick'am!' Tanks yelled, yanking up the abandoned costume. All the while she twisted her waist and danced, her eyes never left him. They were desperate but determined to make him believe her. When she tried to give him back the costume, he refused it. He shook his head and reached into his pockets. He dug inside and pulled out a handful of stuff. 'Thro'way!' he cried again and again as rolls of wire, screwdrivers and rubber bands tumbled to the ground. He wiped his face and danced like his feet were on fire. And with each step, he threw away another useless thing he'd gathered, deceiving himself that it was precious and worth saving.

Chuks charged forward and did his front flip. A roar went through the circle. The crowd began to clap in rhythm as Chuks danced in Jomi's face. His look was bewildered and panicked but he was also determined to fix things. Jomi could see that. Chuks was ready for battle.

'Fix'am!' Chuks yelled and then did his jerky moves.

'Fix'am,' the crowd roared, echoing Chuks. It was thunderous. Jomi felt goosebumps prick his arms at the sound. But it made him even angrier. And when he saw Prosper come up to him, he was already throwing more things on the ground. The floor in the circle was already almost completely covered with his stuff. His rubbish.

The last bit of his heart broke as he kicked stuff aside to dance his last battle. Prosper was already yelling 'Shine'am' and the crowd was already singing '*Shine'am, Shine'am*' along with Prosper's smooth Happy Feet moves. He was definitely shining, Jomi thought sadly. They would have been so good on that *LLD* stage. And holding his mum would have felt so good too.

The last of his energy sizzled out of his bones along with his last belongings. Jomi dropped his arms to his sides, suddenly feeling hollowed out and lost in the midst of the wild crowd. He ignored Destiny's Crew trying to hand him the costume and took a last glance at the entrance.

Chewing-gum man and the other uniformed men were breaking into the tight circle. They were pushing people out of the way and looking very angry.

The world swayed as Jomi was heaved into the air by Chuks and Prosper for the final dramatic move that they would never get to show on stage. Jomi's belly lurched with the sensation of falling as they dropped him to the ground where Tanks had done her split.

The roar from the crowd was so loud, his ears hurt. Jomi grabbed his rucksack and stumbled away. He pushed past someone holding a phone into his face. It was Hassan. Had he been filming the whole thing? 'You guys were fantastic!' he said, with a wide grin.

Hassan hadn't understood anything. Didn't he get what this was about?

Jomi raced around groups of people, back up to the road.

'Wait, Jomi,' Tanks called.

He slowed.

Chuks and Prosper caught up with them. They looked back fearfully to see if the guards were coming after them.

Luckily the guards were too busy getting the crowd back in line. No one was coming.

Hassan caught up. 'Wawu your dance was faya, ahn-ahn, so much pepper and emotion, I was moved to the bone, man. Well done!' He grinned and clapped like Jomi's life hadn't just been ruined. He hadn't even realized what had happened. 'I need to check out the video, man,' he said, finding a spot on the ground. He started scrolling on his phone.

'We have to wait here,' Tanks gasped, catching her breath. 'Aunty Bisi said we weren't to leave the premises. We are to wait here for Mr Folarin.'

Jomi hadn't even really listened to those instructions. He had never thought beyond performing at *LLD* and meeting his mum here. He'd never imagined what he'd do if she didn't come. If they didn't even get to perform.

Again and again he'd imagined her seeing him live on TV, then jumping into a bus or taxi and coming all the way to the LLD Plaza to get him. That was all. Full stop. End of his imagination.

Now all his plans and dreams seemed ridiculous. Completely improbable. What had he been thinking?

The whole idea of finding his mum in Lagos was absurd. He'd never in his life felt more stupid.

He really was useless. He wasn't useful to anyone. He had been a burden to his uncle and aunty. He was a burden to his mum as well, that's why she hadn't taken him along with her. He was a burden to Aunty Bisi. She was at her limit. He was one too many and they all knew it.

He looked at his new-found friends and his

heart, already pummelled like a lump of pounded yam, felt even more bruised as he realized what he had to do.

He looked around him. At the skyline of the tallest buildings he'd ever seen. The night was pitch black against their glowing outlines. The bright square windows in the buildings looked like gems lined up in perfect rows. The skyline was otherworldly and beautiful in a wicked kind of way. Like a crowd of tall untouchable dreams staring down at him with mean, glittery eyes. Forever too high to be reached.

Lagos was a fraud. Of what use were dreams around every corner if you could never reach them no matter how far you stretched?

It was a city of nightmares.

'I'm leaving Lagos,' he said quietly.

All three of them, Tanks, Chuks and Prosper, stared at him with grave faces. Their eyes filled with tears and even though they looked broken he could see that they understood. Each one of them had been in this situation before. That moment when separation was the only way out. They were used to goodbyes.

One after the other he hugged them without a word.

Tanks held him too tight, not releasing him. He had to pull out of her grip. And without looking back, he ran off into the night.

## CHAPTER 37

# ALL IS LOST

All Jomi wanted was to get away from the bright lights and tall buildings. Away from the fakeness. Away from the dreams that were only for rich people even though they already had more than enough. He slowed down when his chest began to feel like it was filled with razor blades and not lungs.

He felt hollowed-out and strange. His steps were much too quiet. His empty pockets rubbed against his thighs like sad wrung-out socks. He missed the clanking of his things. But he knew he was never going to pick up anything ever again. What was rubbish, was just rubbish.

As soon as he slowed down, Ghost popped her head out of the gourd on his back and nuzzled into his neck.

'It's over, Ghost. I've given up.'

He stroked her back, but went rigid when his fingers sank into a gap. He hurried to a street light and examined her more closely. Her fur was thinner and she had bald patches everywhere.

'Oh no, Ghost!' She was gazing at him and his sad eyes were reflected in hers. 'We need to get you a new home. A real forest home.' It was just as well, since he was leaving Lagos. He would find her a forest. The thought of letting her go was too much to bear at the moment, so he nuzzled his face into her fur and pushed the thought aside for now.

He walked until the roads became cosier and greener, framed by tall, old trees that swayed in the night breeze. He passed the high gates of rich people's houses. Houses with huge windows, large enough for people passing to look inside and see all the things they would never have. Houses that smelt of fresh paint and perfumes. Houses which sat squarely on juicy green lawns that were lit by alternating beams of powerful floodlights. Floodlights that were never affected by power failures.

He walked on and on until the roads slowly began to have potholes again and the gutters began to fill with green filth again. Even Victoria Island seemed to have its different levels of richness. He reached junctions where hawkers sold palm wine and guguru ati epa and he began to feel more comfortable again. His belly rumbled. He thought of the others. Mr Folarin would come to pick them up later on. They would go back to Aunty Bisi. They would have a place to sleep, regular meals. They would be safe.

His heart fell. He almost turned around. But even if he could have found the way back, he owed it to Ghost to find her a forest somewhere outside Lagos. Tears filled his eyes but he wiped them away quickly.

All he needed was to find a bus stop, or even better a lorry park. He would smuggle himself on to a lorry again and out of Lagos. He would just go anywhere the lorry took him. He would create a new destiny for himself. A new path to walk on. One on which he would have to walk alone.

He staggered to an abrupt halt.

There at the side of the road, dimly lit by a

street lamp, was a bright almost-new naira note. Enough money to get him a delicious steaming portion of moin-moin. His belly groaned and he suddenly had an intense craving for the spicy orange softness of moin-moin, wrapped in banana leaves with juicy fillings of fish and egg chunks.

'Wow, we got lucky,' he said to Ghost as he bent over.

But the word lucky left a bad aftertaste in his mouth. It immediately had him thinking of his mum. *Don't even worry, Jomi. Just let life surprise you, when you are least expecting it.*

Serendipity.

He'd been looking forward to sharing with his mum the word for her special kind of luck.

Was this one of those life's surprises?

He looked at the naira note and felt something hot flare up in his belly.

'First of all, what I am looking for is my mum, not money!' he hissed into the night. As if life, or destiny, or God was somewhere out there listening.

'I don't care about eating any moin-moin now,

if I could have my mum instead.' He was yelling now. Ghost popped back into the gourd with a small frightened chirp.

He folded his arms across his chest.

'I'm not picking this up,' he called.

'If you are out there somewhere, and you left this here for me for a reason, then prove it. I'll go away and come back in thirty minutes. If this money is still here, then I'll know it was here for a reason. Then I'll know it was here just for me to find. And I'll believe everything happens for a reason. And I won't go away to find a new destiny somewhere else. I'll know there may still be hope for me to find my mum here in Lagos.'

He marched off and around the corner. His heart was beating wildly. This was it. A sign.

He walked faster and faster away from the spot for what he felt had to be about fifteen minutes and then he walked back.

The money was gone.

## CHAPTER 38

# TRYING TO KNOW WHAT YOUR DESTINY IS

Jomi paced the side of the road searching for the money. But he knew it was no use. It had been lying directly under the ray of the street lamp.

The street was as deserted as before. It was a less busy side street with hardly anyone passing. And yet, the money was gone.

Pff!

'You see, Ghost? There's no such thing as destiny. Or serendipity. It's all rubbish. Things don't happen for any reasons. They just happen!'

Just as he said it, there was a rumbling sound. A big lorry screeched and came to a halt at the red lights.

'That's it,' he said. 'We're leaving.' He ran as

fast as he could and just like he'd done back home some weeks ago, he jumped on to the back of the truck, latching on to its loading area just when the truck began to move. It was filled to the brim with boxes. Perfect. It looked like this one was leaving Lagos.

'Well, that I call good luck. Plain good old luck. A lorry, passing by when I need it.'

Ghost began twittering wildly. She popped her head out of his rucksack and into his face.

'Shh!' he whispered. 'We'll get caught.' But she wasn't having it. She sounded almost angry and after a loud whirl of twitters, she just sprang off his shoulder.

'Ghost!' he yelled, almost falling off as he twisted backwards to see where she'd gone. Quickly he grasped the metal latch. 'Ghost!' She was a small shadow on a street lamp that was beginning to look smaller every second.

How could she do this to him now! He slid down to the ledge and waited for the lorry to slow. At the next opportunity he jumped off and somersaulted on to the road. An approaching car honked loudly. 'You don crase?' the driver shouted.

Jomi raced back, hissing angrily.

'What is wrong with you?' he called. He couldn't shout as loud as he'd have liked to because just up the road was a little umbrella stand with a woman sitting underneath. Two kids were standing in front of her and she was handing them warm slabs of steaming moin-moin.

The scent of the spicy moin-moin wafted towards him and his belly tightened. He curled up his fists tightly. He should have picked up that money. Then he would have been standing there with them now. Instead, he was hungry and not on a truck on his way out of Lagos to a new destiny.

Nothing was working like he wanted.

'What is your problem, Ghost,' he hissed. 'Look around, there is nothing here! Not even a tree. I thought we wanted to find you a forest? What do you want here?'

She ignored him and just stared ahead.

Jomi looked and his eyes caught something in the distance that took his breath away.

Red letters on the top of a tall tower-like building some blocks away. The letters were broken and blinking oddly as if the lamp inside them was broken.

'SEND PITY' they blinked.

It was the tower! The one his mum could see from her window.

'Ghost!' he whispered. 'Ghost, the tower . . . the lights . . .'

Jomi began to run, up the street towards the tower. Ghost bounded off the lamp post and leapt on his shoulder, latching on tightly. He could feel it in her tense little body, that she was just as excited as he was.

His mum was here. She could be in any one of these houses. She was so close, he could hardly stop himself from calling 'Mum! Mummy! Mum!' all the way up the street.

He stopped briefly to catch his breath and think.

This area here was right, since he could read the red letters. It had to be one of these streets on this side of the tower. He pulled out her letter and held it in the light of a street lamp. His hands were shaking so badly, he had to drop the letter on the floor to read it. She'd mentioned something about the house. He knew there was something she'd said.

There it was!

*I clean one of these fine-fine houses with big*
*bushes of white hibiscus in front.*

He snatched up the letter and pounded the
ground with his heels as he raced up the street.

It turned out not to be as easy as he'd thought,
because the red letters could be seen almost half a
mile away and there were so many streets. And
yet Jomi ran and ran, not tiring. Ghost held on to
his shoulders for dear life. Once in a while she
would leap off and hop along a fence or wall
before jumping back on to his shoulder.

Unfortunately, many of the houses were in
gated estates and he couldn't enter. The security
guards were not very helpful. And some were
angry at being disturbed and gave grumpy replies.

'Get away, dirty pikin,' an old grouchy one
shouted.

Jomi ran away but he wasn't worried. Now
that he knew where his mum was, he would hang
outside on these streets as long as he needed, till
he found her.

The next gated estate was guarded by two security men. Jomi watched them from the shadows, not sure what to do. He'd had enough of big grumpy security guards today. But he wasn't going to let anything come between him and his mum now. Not when he was so close.

He walked up to the little security house in front of which they sat. It was so tiny, it could have been a playhouse for kids and they could have been two bored oversized children.

'Good evening sirs,' Jomi said, trying to sound respectful and friendly at the same time. Ghost popped her head back into the gourd.

'Please sirs, I'm looking for my mum.'

The men did not react. One of them lit a cigarette and the other one continued to hum along to the quiet music coming from a radio on the ground beside them.

'Ehm . . . she lives somewhere around here,' Jomi continued. 'She works as a house help for her madam in one of these houses.'

'If you think I'm going to let you in here, you can forget it,' the smoking one interrupted.

'Her name is Wande,' Jomi finished.

'We don't let unauthorized people in. And if I knew the names of all the house helps working here, then I would be in the *Guinness Book of Records* by now.' The smoking man grinned and white teeth flashed in the darkness.

'Oh . . . sorry to disturb you then,' Jomi mumbled. 'Thank you sirs.'

He was walking back into the shadows when he heard the other man speak quietly.

'Wande always used to talk about her son in the village though?'

Jomi stood as still as a wobbly house of cards.

'Yeah, you're right,' the smoking one said.

'I haven't seen her in a while though. She doesn't come out for her evening strolls any more.'

'Yeah and she got all quiet these past months, didn't she? Wetin do am, I wonder?'

Jomi couldn't breathe. He felt like if he made any sudden movements, even just breathing, the delicate magic of what was happening would disappear into the night air. Everything around him blurred and seemed to be happening in slow motion.

'Hey, boy, how does she look?'

Jomi swallowed. 'She's not very tall and she's very slim. Ehm . . . she smiles a lot.'

The men looked at him like he was not too bright. 'Is that all?'

Jomi thought quickly, trying his best to remember his mum's face. It wasn't like she had any very outstanding features like a very wide or hooked nose, or very small or big lips. She just had a very normal and friendly face. And it was almost three years now, he thought sadly.

'She loves dancing and she watches *LLD* every week,' he said.

'Ahh!' The men laughed. 'Yes, na Wande be dat.'

'Oya, follow me,' the smoking one said.

Jomi stumbled after him into the estate. Could this be really happening?

The man stopped at a tall house, just as grand as the others on the street. But what caught Jomi's attention were three bushes of white hibiscus in front of its high walls.

He almost couldn't take the tension any more. He wanted to yell over the wall for his mum to come quickly.

'Solo!' the smoking man called. 'Abeg help me call Wande.'

'Ahn-ahn, late like dis? You can tell her bye-bye tomorrow morning.'

'Why bye-bye? Tell her she get visitor.'

'Visitor for night?'

'Ehn, na her son be dis.'

'Her son! OK.'

A few minutes later Solo's voice returned. 'She say she no get son for Lagos.'

Jomi felt like screaming.

'I'm her son, Jomi. Please tell her I left my uncle and came to Lagos.'

The pitter-patter of flip-flops hitting the ground suddenly echoed through the night air.

'Jomi?'

It was strange how her voice was so familiar, as if it had just been yesterday he'd heard it last. It was soothing and soft like honey melting in warm ginger tea.

'Mummy,' he cried. 'Mummy!'

And then she was running to meet him and holding him.

She wet him with her tears and said many

things. He couldn't really understand anything. All he could think was that her scent had also not changed.

## CHAPTER 39

# SERENDIPITY OR WHEN LIFE SURPRISES YOU

The front of the big house lit up. Bright light shone into the front garden through a window, and a silhouette appeared.

'Wande!' a sharp voice called.

Jomi's mum froze. She put a finger to her lips and Solo hastily made a sign for the other security guard to leave.

'Yes Ma!' Wande replied.

'What is going on out there?'

'Nothing Ma, I'm just talking to Solo.'

'Well, you are disturbing me. Get back to your quarters.'

'Yes Ma.'

Jomi's mum grabbed his hand and led him quickly past the house through a back garden to a smaller building at the end.

'She mustn't know you are here. She wouldn't allow it.'

His mum's room was tiny. Considering the size of Madam's house, Jomi was surprised at how small this room was. A naked bulb shone light on to the narrow bed. Beside the bed was only enough space for an old bedside stool. An empty shelf stood at the foot of the bed with a single bag in it. The rest of the room was empty. No clothes, comb or hair cream. Nothing at all.

'My madam is not a nice woman,' his mum said as if she could read his thoughts.

'I was going to leave tomorrow morning, Jomi. If you had come a day later, we would have missed each other.'

Jomi slipped his hand into hers.

'Oh my goodness, Jomi, I can't believe you are here. I am so happy right now, I don't think you can understand how happy.' She held his face in her hands and smiled her soft smile. 'And how much you've grown!' Her smile suddenly faded. 'Please tell me you didn't actually come to find me all by yourself?'

Jomi bit his lip. 'I had to leave Aunty and Uncle. They couldn't take care of me any more. Bulldozers scattered all the farms and forests.'

His mum's face scrunched up into a worried frown.

'And you didn't come back as you promised,' Jomi added quietly.

'I know, Jomi, I am so sorry. I thought of you, every single day. But I couldn't come back empty-handed. Madam kept on finding reasons why she couldn't pay me. At first, she said it was the best for me because she was keeping the money in a bank for me. Then she started saying things were tight at the moment and she'd had to spend it but she would soon get it back from someone owing her money.

'And do you know what's really sad, Jomi? The money she owes me is really nothing to her. She is so rich. Three years' worth of money for my work will hardly get me far. To her it's a joke, but for me . . . It was all I had.'

His mum took a deep breath. 'Anyway, this evening I made up my mind. I decided to leave without the money. I just wanted to go back to get you. I didn't want to be away from you any longer. So I packed my things. Madam doesn't know yet but I told Solo already.'

She pointed to the bag in the empty shelf.

So, that's why Solo had thought the smoking man had come to say goodbye.

'I will have to start from scratch with nothing to show for three years of work. Madam tricked me into staying another year and another. I was naive and foolish. I fell for it. I have failed you, Jomi. I so wanted to make you proud of me.' His mum's eyes filled with tears.

Now in the light of the tiny room Jomi noticed how thin and fragile she was. Her eyes were not as bright as before. She had dark half-moons beneath them and looked infinitely tired.

Jomi shook his head over and over again. How could she think he would ever be disappointed in her?

'It's not your fault, Mummy. She cheated you!' Jomi crunched his fingers into fists.

His mum shrugged weakly.

'I have not been too well recently. All the worrying made me very sad. I should have left sooner. But leaving felt like giving up. Like giving her the right to keep my money. And also I didn't even have any money for a bus fare home.'

'So how did you plan to get back?' Jomi asked.

'I have been working elsewhere secretly, weaving hair.' She winked an eye. 'Any time Madam left the house for a bit longer, I would rush through my chores and then go out to weave the hair of the other house helps in the estate. And just today I finally got enough money together for the journey back home to get you.'

She turned to face him. 'Imagine if we had missed each other, Jomi! Is it not amazing luck that you came this night? How did you even manage to find me all by yourself?'

'It was the lights,' Jomi said. 'The red lights on the tower . . .'

His mum frowned and then glanced through her curtains. She jumped up abruptly and ripped them apart.

'The lights are out,' she gasped.

Jomi jumped up and peered out. Everything was dark, just the rooftops of the estates and the dark silhouette of the tower standing out against the sky.

'They've never gone out before,' she said. 'Those lights. I always felt like they wanted to tell me something. Those words "send pity" were so annoying. But I couldn't figure out what the complete word was. And I always had the weird feeling it was important for me to know it.'

She glanced at him in disbelief. 'And you say these lights led you here?'

'They were on earlier and you had written about them in your letter. That's how I found you. I didn't have your address.'

'Really?'

Suddenly there was a bright flash. The top of the tower lit up with a red glow. Jomi was blinded and had to blink a couple of times. Then he read it. This time all the letters were alight and finally the full word showed.

*SERENDIPITY*, and beneath, another word: *HOTEL.*

The word was Serendipity!

'Mum, that's the special word I have been wanting to tell you about,' he cried.

They looked at each other and his mum looked just like he felt. Like laughing and crying at the same time. Happy tears. He sat her down on the bed and told her about serendipity. And then he told her everything that had happened. Starting with how he found Ghost.

Ghost popped out her head as soon as she heard her name. Mum giggled in surprise and Ghost snuggled into her lap as if she'd also been waiting all this while to finally meet her.

And while his mum cuddled Ghost, Jomi told her of how he stowed away in the truck and came to Lagos. He told her of Tanks, Chuks, Prosper and the others. Of Aunty Bisi and the auditions. Of how hopeless he'd been and how he'd almost given up and then finally found her.

She kept on nodding her head, with tears in her eyes like everything just made sense.

And Jomi realized that it really all did make sense now.

'But what will we do now?' he asked later on. They were lying side by side, squashed like two happy sardines in her tiny bed. He'd let Ghost out to search for her dinner in Madam's garden.

'We'll face tomorrow when tomorrow comes,' she replied. 'I'm sure we'll find a way.'

She sat up. 'You know what, now that you're here, Jomi, I feel I can do anything. I am ashamed to admit it, but I had totally lost my will to fight. But seeing you here has brought back the life into my body. I am ready to fight again. Tomorrow morning, I will talk to her again. I will make her give me my money! I am so proud of you, Jomi. You have been so brave. I want to be brave like you.'

Jomi felt something swell inside of him. He wouldn't have been surprised if the room lit up and began to glow because of him.

A loud buzzing sound ripped through the darkness.

His mum stiffened and Jomi sat up beside her. 'What was that?'

His mum was already getting up. 'It's Madam.'

'What? Is that how she calls? What does she want from you?'

'Probably a glass of water or sometimes she wants a massage when she can't sleep.'

'But it's probably past midnight? Can't she get her water herself?'

'That's the job, Jomi,' she said quietly. She switched on the light, grabbed a key that hung on a rope beside the door and slipped into her flip-flops.

Jomi still sat rigid with the shock of the loud buzzing bell. For a few seconds he glanced at the door out of which his mum had just slipped. Then he tiptoed out after her. He was much too nervous to stay in the room. He wanted to try to get a glimpse of this madam. His mum opened the back door and went into the house. The light was already on and Jomi immediately heard voices.

He sneaked closer.

'Madam, I have something to tell you. I will be leaving tomorrow. I have packed my bags. I need to take care of my son. He needs me. I will need my money.'

'Wande, please not this again,' a sharp voice replied. 'Just make me a tea, so I can sleep.'

'Madam, I have worked almost three years for you. I have earned that money and I want it!'

'Oh goodness, Wande, you can't seriously want to have this discussion now! It's past midnight!'

'If it's not too late to wake me up just to make you a cup of tea, then it is not too late to talk about the money you owe me.'

'What money?'

'What do you mean, Madam? My wages for three years of work.'

'I don't know what you're talking about, I don't owe you anything.'

Jomi slapped his hand across his mouth to stop the gasp from splurting out. What a witch this madam was!

After a brief silence his mum spoke. Her voice was almost a whisper. 'Madam, please, you cannot be serious! I worked hard for you. This is not fair.'

'I don't know what you mean. We agreed on three years of lodging in exchange for your services.'

'You know that's not true, Ma.'

'Show me a contract in which anything otherwise is written.'

'But you said there was no need for a contract. You said you didn't do contracts because you believed in trust.'

'Well, maybe next time you should think twice before trusting someone you don't know.' Madam's voice was like a jagged knife ripping painfully through the quiet night.

His mum shrieked and Jomi couldn't bear the pain in her voice.

He grabbed the door handle and pushed the door so hard it crashed into the wall.

# CHAPTER 40

# THE SINISTER FORESTS OF EGBERE

'You are a liar and a cheat. A mean person who takes advantage of others in need.' The words burst out of Jomi as if a tap had been switched on full force.

'Jomi!' His mum stared at him, wide-eyed. Then she held out a hand for him to come closer. They were standing in the largest and shiniest kitchen he had ever seen in his entire life.

Madam was a round woman wearing a hairnet and a silky kind of robe tied with a knot around a wide waist. She had a mean kind of face that fit perfectly to her voice, with small cat-like eyes that were a little too close to each other and a large nose. She stared at him for a minute, too stunned at his sudden appearance to speak.

'What . . . who is this?'

'This is my son Jomi. He came to find me.'

Madam eyed Jomi, scrunching up her big nose like she'd smelt ten-day-old bean porridge. Then she glanced back at his mum, her eyes narrowing. 'Like I said, I don't know anything about any money. But you are free to take your little brat with you,' she glanced at him with a frown, 'and go. Thank you for your services.'

'Thank you for your services?' Now his mum lost it. Her chest heaved deeply and the words burst out of her like angry bullets. 'I am not going anywhere until you give me my money.'

'Suit yourself,' Madam said. She picked up a green bottle on the counter, poured red liquid into a wine glass and turned to leave. 'Just make sure you leave my tea on the counter and close the door when you go; you know I don't like any stray cats coming in.'

Jomi's belly lurched at her words. She'd just given him an idea.

He began to make his whistling noises.

Madam, who was about to leave the kitchen, stopped in her tracks.

Ghost bounded in through the open back door and into the kitchen as if she'd already sensed something was amiss. She leapt across the counter and up on to the large shiny fridge, then across the sink and on to his shoulder.

'Haaa!' Madam yelped. 'Get that thing out of here.'

His mum glanced at him with questioning eyes.

'Solo! Solo!' Madam called frantically. She stumbled backwards over her long robe and fell heavily on her bum.

His mum ran forward to help her up. Madam had spilt the wine on herself but didn't even care about it. Her eyes didn't leave Ghost.

'What . . . what in heaven's name is this monster?'

'It's a bushbaby!' Jomi replied.

Madam shrieked.

'I brought her from the sinister forests of Egbere. We people from Egbere land can sense it when our people are in trouble. Our chief sent me with this bushbaby to help me get my mum back.'

'You can have your mum back, please take her

back to Egbere land as quickly as possible,' Madam cried.

Jomi was beginning to enjoy himself. He deepened his voice and continued in a foreboding, dark tone. 'Yes, but she cannot return empty-handed. If she does, the bushbaby will not be appeased.'

Jomi moved towards Madam and she edged backwards into her fridge, whimpering.

'Have you ever heard a bushbaby cry at night?'

Madam shook her head and tears began to leak out the sides of her eyes.

He twittered to Ghost and she gave a loud twitter in response and ended with the most petrifying baby howl.

'Ooooh,' Madam wailed, almost sounding like a baby herself.

'One cry is not enough, but if a bushbaby cries outside your window for one whole night, then you know what will happen right?'

Madam closed her eyes and nodded frantically. Most people had never seen a bushbaby before, but everyone knew the hair-raising stories about them.

'By the break of dawn,' Jomi continued, 'the person will have turned mad and all their riches will be gone!' Jomi only just managed not to grin as Madam's face completely gave way.

His mum stifled a strange cough beside him.

Madam was hyperventilating by now.

'Yes . . . yes . . .' She kept nodding. 'I mean no . . . no . . . please!' she mumbled.

Solo appeared in the doorway. 'Yes Ma!' he said. His eyes widened when he saw Ghost.

'Na wetin be dis?' he asked. Ghost did another round of wailing and Solo moved a step backwards. 'Madam, you want me to do anything?'

Madam glanced at Ghost and then at Jomi. Jomi raised an eyebrow and Madam shook her head quickly. 'No, please go, Solo.'

Solo hurried away.

'I . . . I have money in the safe,' Madam whimpered and stumbled out of the kitchen. She kept jerking around every few steps to see if Ghost was following her. Muffled mumbling and hiccuping sounds came from inside the house, some shuffling, and then a beeping sound.

His mum covered her mouth and was looking

at him with eyes ready to plop out of her head.

Then she gripped the counter tightly as if she wasn't sure she could stand without support.

Jomi was nervous too. Worried. Madam could call someone for help. The police. She could change her mind.

But she came back quickly, clutching bundles of money to her heaving chest.

'Please . . . please take this.' She snatched up a black leather handbag from a stool and emptied out the contents. Lipsticks, a handkerchief, keys and some other things clattered on to the table.

She stuffed the money into the bag and handed it to Jomi's mum with hands that were trembling so hard, the whole bag was trembling along with her.

'This should cover the three years.' Then she glanced fearfully at Ghost. 'I even added some more for the wonderful services,' she said to the bushbaby.

Ghost was busy marking her territory in the kitchen by peeing on the highest point, which was the fridge. The shiny silver of the fridge turned golden for a brief moment.

Madam whimpered. 'Ehm . . . s-s-sorry, bushbaby, sorry Wande, it was just a misunderstanding. A terrible misunderstanding.'

Jomi's mum nodded, took the handbag and walked out.

Jomi twittered for Ghost to follow and she bounded after him, leaving golden-yellow prints all over the counter.

## CHAPTER 41

# WHEN YOUR CUP OF LUCK IS NO MORE EMPTY

'We're almost there,' Jomi's mum said with one of those smiles he'd missed so much. They'd just stepped out of the taxi, which was still waiting for them on the main road. His mum clutched Madam's handbag, in which she had also tightly stuffed her few belongings. They left the lit main road behind them and walked on to a darker side road, and his mum leant over to glance into his rucksack to see what Ghost was up to. Ghost immediately popped out and on to Jomi's shoulder, twittering quietly.

'There it is, look,' she said, pointing. Further down, Jomi recognized the looming outline of a forest stretching out to the horizon.

A sign read: 'Welcome to Lekki Conservation

Centre.'

Jomi pressed his cheek into Ghost as soon as he saw it.

She'd seen the forest already and was making little excited noises.

Suddenly a long wail sounded from inside the forest. Ghost went totally still and then replied in a loud chitter of wailing and trilling.

She bounded off his shoulders and down the road.

'Bye Ghost!' Jomi called, trying his best to sniff away his tears. She skidded to a halt, came back and leapt on to his shoulder again.

'Thank you, Ghost,' he said, his eyes so full of tears he could hardly see her. 'For being my friend and for helping me.' He leant into her one last time. Then he twittered and chirped as she sped off to her new home.

His mum's arm curling around his shoulder comforted him as they walked back to the taxi.

In all directions, the city was alive and dancing with energy. As the taxi drove through the streets, hawkers still flitted about and street junctions were as lively as ever, with flickering fires grilling early morning bole, music playing and people chatting in low voices. Here and there power failures had sent some areas into temporary darkness. But even in those places, little specks of light moved through the dark patches as cars or motorcycles found their ways home. Houses lit up here and there with generators or lanterns.

Lagos really never slept. He found himself warming to the city again. In the end, he had found his dream here.

'Do you think our destiny is going to finally wake up now?' Jomi asked.

His mum looked at him in surprise. 'Jomi, she is already wide awake and working hard to fulfil her plan. She woke, when you set out to look for me with nothing but three letters in your pockets. Do you know how unlikely it was to find me? And yet you did. How do you think that happened? And all the helpers you had: Ghost, Tanks, Aunty Bisi and the others. Their destinies all crossed with yours because you set out on that journey to find me. Their destinies have also been changed by you in some way.'

'Oh,' Jomi said, feeling overwhelmed. Had he

really caused all that to happen? 'But I still don't understand how destiny actually works,' he said.

'I think being given a destiny is like being given paper and some crayons. You have to draw out your own life for yourself.'

Jomi looked at her. 'What do you mean?'

'Some people get a large palette of colours and they could easily draw the most beautiful futures for themselves. If they wanted to. But not everyone makes the best of what they are given, you know.'

Jomi nodded.

'People like us only got a few stubs of crayons or only a single pencil to draw out our future. So, it is a bit harder. But you know what, Jomi, I have seen the most beautiful drawings, made with only a single pencil.'

His mum glowed as she said this. Jomi couldn't take his eyes off her.

'And that's exactly what we are going to do. We are going to draw the most beautiful picture with that one pencil we've got.'

She winked. 'I'm sure life still has one or two surprises for us.'

He smiled, feeling like his insides might soon burst.

'We're going to make it happen, Jomi,' she said, clutching his hand tightly.

And he believed her.

# RADIO ANNOUNCEMENT

**G**ood morning, Lagosians, and welcome to our weekly recap of Lagos stories.

A video filmed at the LLD Plaza in Victoria Island has gone viral since Nneka Oji, the moderator of the show, called out to Lagosians to find the children dancing in the clip.

Following an unfortunate event at the Plaza in which street urchins were turned away at the auditions which were meant to be accessible to anyone and everyone, the children danced outside of the premises and were filmed by a friend. In an amazing and heartfelt show of creativity and passion, the kids danced their grief at being thrown out.

Nneka Oji, now a huge fan of the kids, said it

*was the most impressive and heartbreaking dance she had ever seen.*

*Any hints to the whereabouts of the children would be appreciated and rewarded personally by Nneka herself.*

*Now Lagosians, if you haven't seen the dance yet, do yourself a favour and check out hashtag #DestinysCrewLagos or hashtag #LLDWonder.*

*I can't wait to see what happens next. Nneka was secretive about her plans for the children but knowing her, I'm sure it will be something fantastic.*

*And by the way, what a wonderful name the children chose for themselves. Destiny's Crew. Is it serendipity that got these kids discovered by LLD star presenter Nneka Oji, known for her own tough but successful rise out of poverty to stardom?*

*My Lagos people, if you ask me, this sounds very much like a story of destiny awakening.*

# ACKNOWLEDGEMENTS

This book was written in a very short and intensive burst of time during which I went into almost complete reclusion. My first and biggest thank you goes to my daughters for their patience and their sweet attempts at cheering me on – home-baked cookies and all. You are my biggest joy and inspiration, always.

To my dear family for unfailingly being there for me, and with so much cheerleading. I am a blessed daughter, sister, aunty and sister-in-law.

A heartfelt thank you to my super brilliant editor Rachel Leyshon, for immediately loving Jomi and his friends and for that awesome note.

To Jazz Bartlett Love and Olivia Jeggo for always having my back in the UK and to Elinor Bagenal – getting those good-news emails from you is always so special! Thank you also Rachel Hickman for making this gorgeous cover possible and Barry Cunningham for the lovely book intro, again.

Laura Myers, you have been so patient with me, thank you for your last shine'am touches.

Also, many thanks Sarah Wallis-Newman and Esther Waller for your support and for how you and the other lovely Chickens were all so kind when I was stranded for days in that (luckily) rather lovely hotel in Frome.

To Adamma Okonkwo for the brilliant copy-edits and thank you James Catchpole, for your invaluable sensitivity advice. I'm so glad we met!

Thank you Micaela Alcaino for so beautifully bringing Jomi and his crew to life with this absolutely awesome cover.

Big hug for my agent Clare Wallace, thank you for championing me out there and for your kind encouragement when I needed it.

I am also greatly indebted to Othuke Ominiabohs at Masobe books; thank you for your advice and enthusiasm, for our lovely meeting in Lagos and for sharing your inspiring thoughts with me.

Massive thanks to Mat Tobin for having his upcoming teachers read my book as part of their syllabus and for all the work he does in promoting diverse children's literature in teaching.

To all my author friends, many of whom I

befriended through social media. I have been overwhelmed by how supportive of each other authors can be. You have all made me feel like part of a wonderful community in one way or another. Thank you Richard Pickard, Tanja Mairhofer, Alexandra Page, Lindsay Galvin, Jasbinder Bilan, Marie Basting, Emily Randall-Jones, Holly Rivers, Rachel Faturoti, Nina Basovic Brown and Tola Okogwu.

To all my enthusiastic readers – kids and adults, librarians, bloggers, vloggers, teachers like the awesome Kevin Cobane and booksellers like the lovely Ayesha @mirrormewrite.

A very special thank you to those who have shared how much they loved my books. My heart fills with joy when my stories bring smiles, tears, mind-opening thoughts, sparks of recognition and, most of all, a sense of belonging to my readers. There is hardly a greater fulfilment.

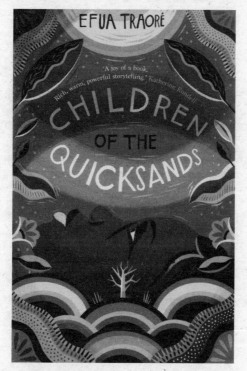

**CHILDREN OF THE QUICKSANDS**

Simi is sent to stay with her long-lost grandmother in a remote Nigerian village. There's no TV, internet or phone. Not a single human sound can be heard at night, just the noise of birds and animals in the dark forest.

Her grandmother makes herbal medicines for the villagers, but she won't talk to Simi about their family's past. Something bad must have happened, but what? To find out, Simi goes exploring.

Caught in the sinking red quicksand of a forbidden lake, her extraordinary journey begins...

'A joy of a book. Rich, warm, powerful storytelling.'
KATHERINE RUNDELL

Paperback, ISBN 978-1-913322-36-6, £7.99  •  ebook, ISBN 978-1-913696-05-4, £7.99